BIG AIR

A PODIUM SPORTS ACADEMY BOOK

LORNA SCHULTZ
NICHOLSON

JAMES LORIMER & COMPANY LTD., PUBLISHERS
TORONTO

James Lorimer & Company Ltd., Publishers acknowledges the support of the Ontario Arts Council. We acknowledge the financial support of the Government of Canada through the Canada Book Fund for our publishing activities. We acknowledge the support of the Canada Council for the Arts which last year invested $24.3 million in writing and publishing throughout Canada. We acknowledge the Government of Ontario through the Ontario Media Development Corporation's Ontario Book Initiative.

Library and Archives Canada Cataloguing in Publication

Schultz Nicholson, Lorna, author
    Big air / Lorna Schultz Nicholson.

(Podium Sports Academy)
Issued in print and electronic formats.
ISBN 978-1-4594-0530-1 (bound).--ISBN 978-1-4594-0531-8 (pbk.).--
ISBN 978-1-4594-0532-5 (epub)

    I. Title. II. Series: Schultz Nicholson, Lorna. Podium Sports Academy.

PS8637.C58B52 2013   jC813'.6   C2013-904189-3
C2013-904190-7

James Lorimer & Company Ltd.,
Publishers
317 Adelaide Street West, Suite 1002
Toronto, ON, Canada
M5V 1P9
www.lorimer.ca

Distributed in the United States by:
Orca Book Publishers
P.O. Box 468
Custer, WA, USA
98240-0468

Printed and bound in Canada.

Manufactured by Friesens Corporation in Altona, Manitoba, Canada in August 2013.
Job # 87636

CHAPTER ONE

"One more time, Jax!"

I gave Rob a thumbs-up before I pulled my goggles down to cover my eyes. I inched my snowboard forward and got into the right position at the lip of the half pipe, a U-shaped bowl that allowed us riders to do jumps and tricks as we moved from wall to wall. I was going to perform the jump called a McTwist, and Rob Findley, my good friend and fellow snowboarder at Podium Sports Academy, stood at the bottom with my video camera to catch my action. To do the McTwist — an inverted 540-degree flip — I had to go off my heel-side wall.

"I'm recording!" Rob yelled from the bottom of the half pipe.

Adrenalin surged through me. My body vibrated and my nerves buzzed. I loved the rush that flooded through me just before I was to jump. I sucked in a deep breath, exhaled, and made my move. I cruised off the wall, trying to get speed, down to the horizontal flat, through the transition area and up the other side wall. My speed dictated how much air I would get at the top of the wall. To take air I would fly past the height of the wall and into space. It was the key to success. My speed launched me upwards of ten feet and into free space. At exactly the right time, I twisted my body, and the airborne feeling of being in that nothing space charged through me. I completed the inverted 540-degree move and landed on the flat with my knees bent to absorb the shock. I went up the other side, slowed down, and headed toward Rob.

"Awesome!" yelled Rob.

I cruised over, unhooked the bindings on my board, and stepped out. "Let me see," I said. I lifted my goggles.

"You nailed it," he said.

I had also taken video footage from a special camera that went on the top of my helmet, but I wanted both angles so I could edit. We reviewed the video and I nodded. "That's the best one yet. Thanks. I really appreciate your help."

"Hey, no problem. Anytime."

The video was for my sponsor, Burton Boards, and I really wanted to show them that I had perfected some new jumps. They had signed me last year and with the signing came the responsibility not only to compete and do well in contests but to keep upping the ante. They also had this policy that I be a good advocate for their products. In other words, keep clean.

That I didn't have a problem with. I'd never done drugs and the one party where I'd secured some alcohol had been a disaster. I wouldn't relive it if you paid me. Fortunately, that had happened before my sponsorship and it was all in the past. I'd never even had a speeding ticket.

Rob handed me the video camera before he dramatically

blew on his hands. "I swear it's dropped five degrees in minutes," he said.

I peeled my glove off and took my video camera from him before I looked at the grey sky. "Yup, but snow is coming."

"I heard big dump." Rob rubbed his hands together. "We need to get to the hill for some powder and free board skiing. Trees, dude."

"Oh yeah."

Podium's snowboarders practiced at Winsport, which was located in the foothills of the Rockies, in Calgary, Alberta. It used to be called Canada Olympic Park because it was the home of the 1988 Olympics, but since then it had changed names. And although the half pipe was decent, there was nothing like hitting the Rocky Mountains for some real freestyle boarding. I grew up in Quebec, so my hill when I was young was Mont Tremblant. Yes, it was a great hill, but when it snowed in the Rockies the fresh snow was superior.

"Maybe after the weekend," I said. "After our first contest. Once it's done, let's go to Lake Louise." I snapped the lid on the lens and stuck the small video camera in the pocket of my beige-plaid snow jacket. It was from Burton too. They had supplied me with boards and apparel. When I got to Podium, I learned pretty quickly that performance videos were important to get sponsors to look at you. It had taken me a month of lessons, teaching little kids how to snowboard, to buy my two video cameras.

"I'd skip school to hit some fresh powder." Rob grinned. Then he playfully punched my shoulder. "When snow hits, we go."

"Skipping means so much homework." I groaned. "I can't wait to graduate. Next year I'm going to Whistler to train, compete, and teach."

"I'm with ya on that one," said Rob. "Well, except the teaching part."

My phone buzzed in the side pocket of my snow pants and I wondered who was calling me. Maybe Carrie, my girlfriend? Nah. Couldn't be her. She'd told me she had a long synchro practice tonight and that meant hours. Carrie was on Podium's synchronized swimming team, and where I could do flips on land, she did crazy things underwater.

Rob held up his hand and said, "Here's to our first contest of the season and to winning and to making Canada's High Performance Program. We can do it, y'know."

I grinned and slapped Rob's hand.

My phone buzzed *again*. I ripped open the Velcro on my pocket and yanked it out. After I checked the number and saw it was an unknown, I shoved it back in my pocket. Never answer an unknown.

And that's when Rob's phone buzzed. He took one quick look at his, answered a text, and said, "Well, dude, I'm heading out. Mrs. Marino has dinner firing. Meet ya there?"

I nodded. "Yeah, I'm done here too."

My phone buzzed again.

Rob laughed. "Bet that's her. Telling you the same thing as me." Rob rubbed his stomach. "She said lasagna this morning."

I laughed, pulled out my phone, and nodded. "Yup," I said. "Dinner's ready."

"Yes!" Rob pumped his arm.

I playfully shoved him. "Go. I'll meet you there."

Rob loved to eat and our billet mom was the best cook ever. He had just moved in with me this year, as he'd had some issues with his previous billet family: they had served him packaged food and no fresh vegetables or fruits, plus they took vacations all the time and were never home. Bad situation. But now we were roommates.

We both felt as if we'd won the lottery with the Marino family. Rob had been placed with me because the basement of the sprawling Marino bungalow was huge and empty. The Marinos had four children, all boys, and three were at university. Their youngest son, Daniel, was in grade eight and he was a great kid, and a fantastic soccer player. His goal was to also attend Podium, thus the reason the Marinos were keen to billet two of us.

"Thanks again, bro," I said. "I'm going to download tonight and send."

"You owe me." He held up his thumb before he turned and trudged away, his baggy pants dragging in the snow, making crinkling sounds as he walked. I had to shake my head. Rob had been my first friend at Podium and we were opposites.

When I first started boarding back in Quebec and winning contests, so many people, including my father, told me to keep at it. But I didn't fit the profile. I liked country music, kept my hair short and, well, I had definitely inherited my dad's Cree looks. There weren't many of us First Nations kids on the snowboarding circuit. I'd never lived on the reserve where my dad grew up because he had moved away to play hockey in the American Hockey League and had never gone back. He married my mom, a white girl, as my Cree grandmother would call her, and they had lived in the city. Now he had an administrative job with the Canadian Football League.

It may all sound okay, but my home life in Montreal definitely had issues. Big issues. Snowboarding had been my escape.

I picked up my board and carried it behind my back. My phone buzzed again and I stopped and checked it — same unknown number. With my phone securely stashed in my pocket and my gloves back on, I rounded the corner to the parking lot. I looked for my beater, a 1995 baby-blue Chevy Impala wallpapered with Burton stickers.

Then I saw it . . . and I also saw my older brother, Marc, sitting on the hood.

I stopped walking. Marc lived in Montreal. When did he get to Calgary? I had no idea he was coming west. His long black hair hung in his signature ponytail down the middle of his back and he wore a baseball hat backwards. From the distance I could see that his leather jacket was worn and his jeans were tattered and dirty.

My blood rushed through me and not in a good way, not how it did when I was flying through the air. No, my blood was starting to heat. I stood still, trying to slow my breathing. Marc's being here couldn't be good. Not good at all.

I saw Rob's car peel out of the parking lot. If I had known my brother was going to randomly show up, I would have asked Rob for a ride home to avoid him.

Was Marc the one phoning me?

How did he get here? He had no money and never did except . . .

I closed my eyes for a second, then started walking. I had to confront him. Anger mounted with each one of my steps as I tramped to my car. And so did panic. It caught in my throat and made me almost gasp for breath. He was here to make trouble. I knew that much.

Control, Jax, control. He's your brother.

"Hey, Marc," I said when I got within earshot. I tried to sound casual and not let him know my heart was racing a million miles an hour. "Whatcha doing in Calgary?" I slid my board on the roof rack of my car.

Marc slid off the hood. "Hey, little brother." He smacked the hood of my beater. "What's with the car?"

"It's a hunk of junk." I refused to meet his eyes. I didn't want to see the glazed look I knew would be there.

He smacked the hood *again.* "You'd think those sponsors of yours would buy you some new Jeep or something."

My hands shook as I tried to hook my board to the roof rack, struggling to stretch the cold strap. Marc remained silent, which unnerved me because I knew he was watching me; I couldn't see the smirk on his face but I could feel it. I yanked the strap, hooked the end of it on the metal bar and finally secured the board. I jiggled it and when I was sure it wasn't going to fly off, I turned to Marc.

"The car runs," I muttered. "That's all I care about."

He held up his hands as if he was super cool and I immediately saw how jittery he was. How long had it been since his last fix? Hours. I'd seen him like this before. Many times.

"What's wrong with you, little bro?" he asked. "I come all the way from Montreal to see you and this is the hello I get? I thought I'd get a big ol' brotherly hug, telling me you're happy to see me. What's it been? Over a year, bro."

I inhaled and blew out the air before I said, "I don't know why you're here. You've never visited before. And you didn't even tell me you were coming."

Marc scratched at his face. "I wanted to surprise you. You only got one brother, y'know."

Out of the corner of my eye I saw a black, new-looking Ford truck idling, smoke billowing out of the exhaust. In it sat three ugly, mean-looking dudes. Marc's friends. I thought I recognized a guy from home. My body trembled.

I jerked my head toward the truck. "Looks like you got some friends who are ready to go. Nice truck, by the way."

He eyed me up and down. "Nice goggles." He nodded his head. "Nice gear. How much all that set y'back?"

"Shut up."

He walked toward me until he was standing right in front of me. Then he reached up and touched my board. "I bet this is worth some cash." He smiled at me, and I noticed he was missing another tooth. "And I bet you got a few of these sitting in your garage. They give you money too? Those *sponsors* of yours? Dad told me all about your new deal."

Suddenly I deflated, inside and out. In all my years growing up, I'd never won. Now I'd moved clear across the country and I still hadn't gotten away. My shoulders sagged and the anger seemed to just hiss out of me. "What do you want from me, Marc?"

He leaned against my car, trying to act casual, but I could see his body shaking. What a stupid question for me to ask. He only ever wanted one thing.

"Can't I just come for a little visit? We're blood. You and me." He winked at me. "Blood." He pointed at his chest, then poked mine, hard. His finger dug into my breastbone. "You're no different than me. Our old man gave us the same Cree blood and we gotta stick together, 'cause ain't no one gonna treat us right except blood."

I looked directly in his eyes. "Why are you here?"

He stepped one foot closer, until our noses were almost touching. His stale, gross cigarette breath hit my nostrils, but I didn't turn my head.

"I wanted to see my little brother. Jax Barren. Famous snowboarder."

"That's a lie."

"It's a free country?" He posed this as a question, a joke, and he laughed at his own words right in my face.

"That it is," I said. I sighed and stepped away from him.

He pulled his cigarettes out of an inside pocket of his jacket. His hands vibrated as he tried to light one. When it sparked, he blew a mouthful of smoke into my face before he offered the package to me. "You want one?"

I shook my head.

Silence hovered over us.

Finally he spoke again. "We're brothers," he said softly. "That's why I'm here."

When I looked into his eyes I saw a glimmer of the old Marc, the one I followed like a puppy when we were kids.

My big brother.

"Barren, let's go!" one of the guys yelled from the black truck.

"Let's catch up tomorrow," said Marc, walking away.

He jumped into the truck and it spun stones as it sped away. I watched until it was out of sight before I got in my beater. My entire body quivered. It took me two tries before I was able to insert the key into the ignition.

CHAPTER TWO

The smell of sizzling cheese and garlic greeted me when I entered the Marinos'. Rob and I had been given a spot in the four-car garage for all our gear, and I had put my board against the wall and changed out of my snowboarding boots and into the moccasins I wore in the house.

When I walked into the kitchen, Rob was sitting at the island counter shovelling in lasagna.

"*Man,* is this good," he mumbled, his mouth full of food.

"Hi, Jax," said Mrs. Marino. "I would have waited but Rob was starving."

I tried to smile. "It's okay." I took a seat on a stool at the huge kitchen island. There were enough stools to seat eight people. The Marinos' designer kitchen was as big as the entire first floor of my house in Montreal. During the week, we ate at the island because Mr. Marino was out of town a lot and Daniel often had soccer practices or workouts. On the weekends, we all sat down at the kitchen table, which could seat at least ten people. I'd never seen such a big house before, but the Marinos lived in an area where everyone had huge houses built on two-acre lots.

Mrs. Marino handed me a plate of food.

"Is that enough?" she asked.

"Oh yeah." It was always enough when she dished up the plate. Like twice as much as enough. "Dude, it's *unbelievable.*" Rob kept his head lowered as he shovelled in another forkful.

We ate in silence for a few moments before Rob sat up straight, patted his stomach, and said, "I'm stuffed. That was amazing, Mrs. Marino."

She smiled. "Rob, you are too easy to please."

Rob got up and went to the sink, rinsing his plate before putting it into the dishwasher. He had just shut the dishwasher door when he looked at me and snapped his fingers. "Hey, forgot to ask. Who was the guy in parking lot? He asked me which one was your car."

I shook my head. "No one." I spoke low. This was not a conversation I wanted to have, especially when he was standing on the other side of the island and I would have to speak loudly to be heard. I had mentioned my dad and sister, Serena, to anyone at Podium who asked. I wanted to forget that I even *had* a brother.

"You gotta know the guy. He knew you." Rob was persistent.

"It was my . . . brother," I muttered. I should have lied. I stared at my plate and picked up a forkful of lasagna. "This looks great." *Change the subject, Jax.*

But no go.

"Your brother?" asked Mrs. Marino. "You've never talked about a brother. I knew you had a younger sister."

Just the word *brother* coming from her mouth made me

lower my head even more and stare down at my plate, at the perfectly melted cheese. I tried to continue eating. Why had I said anything? "He's four years older than me," I mumbled.

"You should have asked him for dinner," she said. "Your family is welcome to come over anytime. You know me, there's always lots of food."

"It's okay," I quickly replied. "I don't think he'll be in town long."

After dinner, Rob and I went downstairs, into our basement "lair," as he called it. Complete with a pool table, air-hockey table, and a flat-screen 52-inch television set, the place was a dream house and the basement was basically ours. I immediately went to my room and got my laptop, then took it back out to the big open recreation room and settled in front of the television. I wanted to view my video again and fix it up with sound and some special effects so I could load it onto YouTube and mail the link to my sponsors. And I could do that while watching television — *Breaking Bad* to be exact. Rob and I were repeating the episodes. Rob had also found his way to the sofa with his laptop and was obviously doing homework by the books spread out everywhere. He was amazing at doing homework and watching television at the same time.

We both worked for an hour without saying too much of anything to each other. Finally I sat back and said, "Wanna watch my video before I upload and send?"

"Sure. Anything to get away from math."

He sat beside me and leaned in to watch the sixty seconds

of video, nodding the entire time. "It's good," he said when it was over. "Must've been the cameraman."

I laughed and playfully punched his arm before my phone buzzed. Immediately my heart raced. Was it my brother? When I glanced down and saw Carrie's name and a text message, my heart slowed down as if I'd done a full stop on my snowboard.

"gonna pop by to see video"

I quickly replied.

"k"

The Marinos lived in the foothills west of Calgary, in an area called Foothills Way. Rob and I were a five-minute drive from the school. Bonus. Especially for sleeping in before school started. Since Carrie's practices were usually at the pool at the school she often popped in on her way home. The doorbell rang within ten minutes. I heard the door open and Mrs. Marino usher Carrie inside. Their murmuring voices carried down the stairs, but I couldn't hear what they were saying. Mrs. Marino loved it when Carrie came over because then she had another female in the house. Their voices continued for a few minutes, then I heard the padding of footsteps.

"Thanks, Mrs. Marino," said Carrie from the top of the stairs.

Carrie came down the hardwood stairs, and when she hit the landing she said, "Hey Jax, Rob."

Rob acknowledged Carrie with a thumbs-up.

Carrie plopped down beside me on the sofa, our shoulders and legs touching, and said, "Play it for me."

I pressed PLAY again on my computer and we watched the video. When it was over she said, "That is so cool. I can't believe you can flip like that."

"Yeah, and without nose plugs," I teased, bumping my shoulder into hers.

Carrie and I had only been going out for a month. Last year she had gone out with Aaron Wong, a guy from the hockey team. He was a cool guy and I liked him a lot, so I took it slow with her, in case he still liked her. But he pretty much gave me the go-ahead when he started hanging out with a girl from the volleyball team. Carrie and Aaron were now friends, which made life a lot easier because we had a lot of the same friends.

I also took it slow with Carrie because she was my first girlfriend. The entire relationship thing was new to me and I wasn't sure what to expect. At first I'd been worried she'd be clingy, but Carrie wasn't like that at all. The last thing I wanted was a hovering girlfriend. No thanks. I figured if I wanted to go snowboarding for the day, I'd just go.

So far, so good, though.

My phone, which was beside Carrie on the sofa, buzzed. She picked it up and handed it to me. I glanced at the number and when I saw it was unknown, I tossed the phone onto the cushion beside me. If Carrie was curious about who it was, she said nothing.

"What episode is this?" She pointed to the television.

"Third show, first season," replied Rob without looking at either of us or the television.

"First season is my fave," she said.

"Me too," I said.

"Oh, by the way, I found out today I have the weekend off. Yes!" She cheered using her hands. "Just one early-morning practice on Saturday. So Allie and I are coming to watch you guys this weekend. She's doesn't have any games either."

"That's great," I said.

"I'm so jacked!" said Rob with more enthusiasm than I'd shown.

"We have Monday off school too," said Carrie.

"We do?" Rob furrowed his eyebrows and looked totally confused.

I tossed a pillow at him. "Where have you been? It's been in our agendas since September."

Rob's eyes lit up. "Let's hit Lake Louise!"

"I can't," I moaned. "I have to teach all afternoon."

"That sucks," said Rob.

"It's a pretty easy job," I said. "And good money." I shrugged. "I bet I could make a ton one day if I had my own snowboarding school. After I compete in the Olympics, of course."

"Dream big," said Rob. "After *I* compete in the Olympics, I'm going to collect endorsements and own a store. I'd rather do that than teach. I taught at a camp one Christmas," said Rob, laughing. "It was the worst. This little kid got to the top and told me he had to go pee. I told him to pee in the woods."

"You didn't!" Carrie burst out laughing.

"I thought it was a good answer but he started bawling. My boss was ticked off at me. Never again."

"Hey, we should do something Sunday night," said

Carrie. "Have a little get-together." She turned to me and I liked how close she was.

I shrugged. "Sure. That'd be good."

"We'll be done early Sunday," said Rob. "I bet we could have some people over here. Mrs. Marino loves it when we have people at the house."

"You guys, seriously, have the best billet family. I could smell the garlic when I walked in the door."

"I'll run up and ask her," said Rob. He hopped out of his seat and slid across the floor in his socks before taking off up the stairs.

As soon as I knew Rob was out of sight, I put my arm around Carrie. She looked up at me, her blue eyes like pools of warm water. I leaned forward and kissed her softly on the lips. She responded by moving closer to me and placing one hand behind my head, her fingertips lightly touching my neck. Shivers ran up and down my body. Gently I pulled her closer to me and wove my fingers through her long blond hair, which felt like soft downy feathers.

"PDA police!" Rob's voice sounded from the top of the stairs.

Immediately we pulled apart. I leaned back and moaned under my breath, and Carrie hugged her knees to her chest. Beside me my phone buzzed, telling me I had yet another text. I looked down and saw the unknown number. Again. Marc. Was he not going to give up? That was probably the fifth text he'd sent.

What was I gonna do?

Rob bounded down the stairs and jumped over the back of the sofa to get to his seat. "We're good to go," he said, stretching his legs out in front on the matching hassock, crossing them at the ankles. "She'll even make homemade pizza and chicken wings."

Carrie burst out laughing. "Omigod. She would do anything for you."

Rob shrugged before he put hands behind the back of his head in relaxation mode. "She likes to cook, I like to eat. And she loooves me. What can I say?"

"I'll talk to her before I go," said Carrie, "and tell her some of the others can bring some food too."

"Daniel has an indoor soccer game later in the evening," said Rob, "but she said it would be okay if we kept the numbers down. And . . . no alcohol."

"I'm good with that," I replied.

The last get-together — it was before Rob moved in with me — I'd managed to get a little alcohol from an older friend and it hadn't turned out so great. Nothing had got broken or anything, but Allie had got drunk. The Marinos had said they were disappointed, but they were willing to let it go if it never happened again. It hadn't and it never would.

When my phone buzzed again, I put a pillow on it.

Carrie glanced my way. "Someone is really trying to get you."

"It's nobody," I said.

"Obviously not *nobody*."

"Telemarketers," I replied. "They start after six and I can't get rid of them."

"O-kay," she said slowly, as if she didn't believe me.

"Who should we invite?" I asked. I had to get her off the

subject of my caller. I didn't want Carrie knowing I had a brother in town. As of less than an hour ago, only Rob and now Mrs. Marino knew I even had a brother.

"Let's make a list," said Carrie. "Then ask everyone on it tomorrow at school."

I was so glad she'd taken the bait.

CHAPTER THREE

The next day at school, I turned my phone on silent because Marc had phoned me two times in the night. By his voice message at 3:00 a.m., I could tell he was completely out of it. I couldn't concentrate in biology. The circulatory system and all its flow patterns blurred in front of me. So I doodled instead of listening. Eagles. Feathers. How did Marc pay for his flight? I shuddered.

Time dragged and questions kept clouding my mind. I just kept doodling. More feathers and eagles and snowboards too.

"Jax."

I almost jumped out of my seat. I glanced up. "What?"

Carrie stood by my desk. "Class is over."

I shoved my pages into my notebook and gathered up my books.

She frowned. "Are you okay?"

"Yeah. Just tired."

As we walked out she said, "Did you understand that stuff?"

"Um. Yeah. Biology is memorization," I said. I hadn't heard a word, but it was the circulatory system and I was sure I could figure it out.

"I'm lousy at memorizing," she moaned.

I playfully bumped her shoulder just to touch her. "You memorize all those synchro routines, didn't you? And you have *exams* in your sport. Memorization should come easy to you."

"Ha-ha. That stuff I like memorizing." She eyed me. "How come you're so tired?"

Why would she care about me being tired? "We should talk to everyone today. For Sunday night."

"Let's do it at lunch." She reached for my hand and I liked how hers felt warm and soft. The physical part of having a girlfriend was the best part. I gave her hand a squeeze before we hit the junction in the hallway where she went one way and I went the other.

"See you at lunch," I said.

Before I entered my French class, I turned on my phone. I breathed a sigh of relief when I saw there were no new messages. Marc would sleep until late afternoon. That was his schedule. Stay out all night and sleep all day. He'd lost more jobs over the past few years, from construction work to pumping gas. He'd lasted the longest at the gas station because it had been a drug dealer's paradise. Obviously, he was out of work again.

Once again, I couldn't concentrate, but fortunately I was fluent in French. I had purposely taken it for an easy credit. I pulled out my pen and paper and doodled: streams and fish this time.

"*Monsieur* Barren." Mrs. Savoie's voice made me sit up straight.

"*Oui,*" I answered.

I heard the snickers around me. "You're busted," whispered Nathan who always sat behind me. Then he whispered, "What is chapter two about in *Guillaume*?"

Guillaume was the French novel we were studying. Okay, this I could answer. I had read the chapter a few nights ago. I stood up and started speaking fluent French, answering the question. Everyone burst out laughing. Why? I could speak better than anyone in the class. I looked around and saw Nathan splitting his side.

Mrs. Savoie shook her head and held up her hand. "*Assez. Asseyez-vous si vous plait.*"

I did what she asked and sat down. Allie was on my other side and she shook her finger at Nathan. "Not nice," she said to him.

She looked over at me. "You were supposed to ask where to find the milk in the supermarket."

I turned slightly. "I'm gonna get you, Moore," I said under my breath.

Of course, he was still laughing.

Class finally ended and when we were in the hallway, I bodychecked Nathan into the lockers, the crash resounding down the hallway.

"Okay, I give." He leaned against the lockers and held up his hands. "Madame Savoie loves to nail you 'cause she knows you speak better French than she does."

"You didn't have to help her."

"Sorry. I couldn't help myself. But I like the eagle you drew."

Marc and I had spent hours drawing eagles, especially

in the summer months. "I'm starving," I said. "Let's get lunch." I paused. "Oh, and Rob and I are having some people over Sunday night. You wanna come?"

Nathan shrugged. "Sounds good to me."

I refused to look at my phone for the entire lunch period because I wanted to enjoy myself. Mrs. Marino made us the best meat sandwiches, always on these fresh Italian buns. Lunch ended too soon, but I only had one more class. I had a spare last class every day so I could be at the hill by two o'clock. Today I wouldn't board long, because tomorrow we competed.

After lunch, I walked out with Carrie and Rob. "Did you ask Nathan?" Carrie said.

"He's coming," I replied. "Kade and Aaron too."

"We should ask Parm's friend, Sophia, from the girls' soccer team," said Rob. He raised one eyebrow up and down. "She's hot."

"Ya think?" Carrie said.

"So-phi-a." Rob used his hands as if he was Italian when he said this. "Just saying her name is sensual." He kissed his fingers.

I rolled my eyes at him. "I thought she was dating that guy from the rowing team."

"Nope," said Rob, with emphasis on the *p* to make it pop. "They broke up and I know that for a fact. He's not a friend of mine so I don't care about waiting the grace period."

Of course, Carrie wanted to know more about the latest broken relationship, and as she questioned Rob, I pulled my phone out of my pocket and turned it on. No more messages. I blew out a rush of air. Maybe Marc had left town already.

CHAPTER FOUR

Saturday morning I awoke to sunshine, a flawless blue sky and fluffy powder snow: in other words, a snowboarder's dream. The fresh snow would make the runs smoother, sleeker, and just better in every way. My body tingled with excitement.

After downing a fresh fruit smoothie, loaded with protein powder, banana, yogurt, almond milk, and blueberries, I went outside. I started my car to let it warm up. As it idled, I loaded two different boards on the roof rack. I needed the second one just in case. I ran my fingers along my edges and liked how they were sharpened. For half pipe I liked them sharp, and for slope-style I liked them dull. Today was half pipe. I inhaled to smell the fresh wax. Both boards had been waxed to perfection. The smell comforted me, just like the smell of my father's homemade chili.

The sun shone so brightly that I put my sunglasses on. Rob and I always took our own cars to the hill, because we liked to listen to our own music to psych up. He liked rap and I liked country.

With Garth Brooks blasting through my speakers (which

were quality speakers for a crap car) I drove to the hill. I loved the trip to the hill, the anticipation of the day ahead. For me, it was like meditation.

When I arrived, I checked in at the event tent to collect my numbered competitor's bib. I slipped it on and went out to get my favourite board. I had brought new Burton stickers and I proceeded to put them on the board, getting it ready for the contest. It was important for my sponsors that I put on clean stickers.

I was just about ready to hit the lift when my coach, Stuart Henry, walked into the tent. He waved and came toward me.

"How you feeling today?"

"Great," I replied.

He put his hand on my shoulder. "Remember the few little things we worked on this week, especially the timing in your turns, and you'll kill it. Don't rush. Let your body move you through the movement."

I nodded. "Yeah," I said.

"Get a good warm-up."

Stu spotted Rob, then slapped me on the back, and I knew he had to make the rounds and see every one of his boarders. I headed outside, strapped one foot into my bindings and glided over to the chairlift. Before a contest, I didn't really talk to many people, my coach being an exception, and maybe Rob. The lift took me to the top of the hill and I cruised off, did up my bindings, and slid my goggles over my eyes. I jumped up and down a few times on my board before I took off down the hill, making my way toward the half pipe area. On the way down, I tried to hit every jump I could find to get some warm-up air and try a few easy grabs. I had loads of time because I was slated as one of the last competitors to drop.

The contest hadn't started yet, but the practice runs had. I waited my turn by the drop-in mound and once I had the go-ahead from the starter, I dropped into the half pipe, cruised down to the flat bottom and up through the vertical transition area, gaining speed. I got a decent amount of air and performed an easy 360 before landing and speeding up the other side of the half pipe to do a switch, so I could go down the hill on my unnatural foot.

I continued up and down the half pipe, completing grabs and flips. Many were just for warm-up and some were ones I would do in my run. I finished my practice run, feeling good about it, and cruised down to the bottom.

I unstrapped my foot, took it out of my binding, and because time was limited and I wanted to see if I could get another practice run in, I starting hiking back up to the top of the half pipe.

Rob was hiking up as well and I fell into step with him.

"When you dropping?" he asked.

"Thirty-fifth. You?"

"Thirty-second. I saw Dean Delaney. He's got last drop time. Like fortieth."

"He's here?" I frowned.

"Yup."

"Wonder why?" I asked. "It's not like there's any big money if you win." Dean Delaney was from the U.S. and touted to be on their next Olympic team.

"I guess he has relatives who live in Calgary," said Rob. "He's visiting."

By now we were almost at the top. Rock music blared from the speakers mounted beside the half pipe. Music was part of the contest. I turned to look at Rob. "I want to beat him," I said. "Wonder what his run is like."

Rob shrugged. "He didn't give me squat. I bet we both could beat him if we have great runs."

I held up my hand and he smacked it.

I managed to get a few more rides through the pipe before the announcer started calling out names for competitors and they were lined up in preparation to drop. I went to the tent at the top of the drop to await my turn. My nerves always kicked in at this time. I paced a bit and stretched and waited, all the time concentrating on my run.

I visualized every flip and turn. I listened to the sound of my landings, the crunch on the snow. I could feel my legs tighten to absorb the shock. I smelled the fresh wax on my board. And I heard the pounding of the music.

When it was close to my time, I stepped into my board and did up my bindings. I slapped my hands together and jumped a bit.

Finally I heard my name and number and headed over to the edge of the drop. I sucked in a deep breath and waited for the starter to give me the go-ahead. I stared below me and could see every one of my hits, the moves I had planned for my run. Fences surrounded the half pipe, and once I dropped, I had space to move, to show what I was made of. Five judges sat at the bottom of the half pipe waiting to give me a score on flow, creativity of line, technical difficulty, and height. The trick was not to get one jump with height and the others small but to keep them all fairly consistent. I needed at least ten feet of air on each wall. And then there was style. Style was style. It was just something you had or didn't have.

Well, I was going to give them a show.

My style was big air, tight moves, and smooth crisp landings.

I inhaled. I heard my go-ahead and immediately dropped into the half pipe.

I cruised to the top of the lip and caught air, performing an easy 360, knowing my next move was a cab 540 — a mid-air aerial spin — then a 720. I needed to land high on the pipe to generate speed from hit to hit. Loose muscles could cause my nose to dig, and that would make me crash and burn. I hit the wall again and I crouched low and raced up, and when I hit the top I made sure my arms were in the exact right position to spin. Off by one inch and I would have to bail.

I completed the hit and landed. After I had done my first three hits I did a switch, which went smoothly. Then I performed an air to fakie, where I had to switch to my reverse stance. My finale was a crippler — which was basically a backflip 360. I needed speed to complete that final move, and big air, which was hard because by then I was winded.

Big speed. Big air. Come on, Jax!

I sailed upwards, hit the lip, flew as high as I could and flipped. I bent my knees and tensed my thigh muscles for the landing. I used my arms for balance and my landing was good. Better than good. Perfect.

I cruised over the finish line and heard the cheers.

It had been a good run. Most competitions were two judged runs, so for the next run I had a few tricks up my sleeve.

I unhooked my bindings and stepped out of my board completely, put it behind my back and walked to the fence. I wanted to watch Delaney go. Stuart came over to stand beside me.

"That was an excellent run," he said.

"Thanks."

"Next run, I think you should add something. You're riding well today. Your balance seems spot on. Don't be afraid to play a bit. Nothing too daring, just a few tweaks."

"Okay," I said.

We watched three boarders, then I saw Delaney at the top of the pipe. "I'm so surprised he's here," I said to Stu.

"It's a good thing for you," said Stu. "His level is something you should aim for this year."

I glanced at Stu. He must have sensed me looking at him because he turned and gave me a little wink. "Confidence, Jax. You've got the talent. Now focus and let it all go."

I squinted to stare up at the top of the pipe, wanting to see Delaney's speed on his first trick. As usual, he looked cool and confident and, Stuart was right, that was often the key to success: make the judges think you were on top of your game. He performed an easy first move, landing with ease and speeding up the other side. His next move was okay, nothing spectacular, and he hesitated slightly when he landed, so the height on his next flip wasn't super great.

When he finished his run, he sailed across the finish line, flashing his big smile, white teeth and all. Such a showboat. He worked the crowd until he spotted me. His smile wavered for a moment before he turned back to the rest of the crowd to give his final wave.

I waited to see his marks up on the marquee board. When I saw that mine had beaten his, I headed back up to the top of the half pipe for my second run. Sometimes there were eliminations at contests, but today, because it was a smaller contest, each boarder did two runs, and it was the best total combined that won the event.

So far, so good.

As I waited for my turn to drop, I visualized my run in my head, over and over. I would make one adjustment and that was to reverse a few spins. I heard my go-ahead, sucked in a deep breath, and dropped.

Down and up. Way up. I flew up to the top of the pipe and knew my air was perfect. Landing, I sailed forward, again got to the lip, caught my air, and spun the opposite way. Up and down and up and down, I flew through my routine.

When I landed my last hit, I knew my second run had been smoother than the first, and I should get extra marks for degree of difficulty. I cruised across the line and grinned. I couldn't help it! That had been one of the best runs I'd ever done. I waited for my marks and when I saw them I squeezed my hand into a fist and said, "Yes!"

I stepped out of my board.

Rob met me by the fence. "You rocked it," he said, patting me on the back.

"Felt so good," I said.

"You could win this."

I looked up at the marks board. "Yeah, but I have to hold my lead."

Even though I saw Carrie and Allie in the crowd, Rob and I took a position by the fence where we could be alone. We watched the next few boarders come down, and then it was time for Delaney.

Right from his drop he was flying.

"Wow," said Rob when Delaney had done a double cork. "That's gutsy."

"He's going for it," I said, watching Delaney's every movement. I glanced upward as he did a McTwist. He landed perfectly and flew up the other side. When he hit his air he had to have been at least twelve feet in the air.

"Great air," said Rob.

I tilted my head to watch Delaney's body fly upwards. "His arms are off," I said.

"Yup," replied Rob. "I bet he bails."

Delaney landed but his body was too far forward and the nose of his board dug into the snow. His body was flung through the air and he did two somersaults before he catapulted into the fence. Gasps sounded from the crowd. I held my breath until I saw him get up and wipe the snow off his pants. "He's okay," I said, relieved.

"What a lucky dude," said Rob. "That was such a huge bail."

Delaney shook his head and there was no flashy smile.

With slumped shoulders he walked away, not even looking at the screen for his marks. When his numbers did go up, Rob looked at me and held up his thumb. "You won!"

"You came third," I said.

When we heard our names called, Rob and I headed over to the podium and were ushered onto our respective blocks. I stepped up and faced the crowd and that's when I saw him. Marc.

When had he arrived?

Had he seen my run? My heart quickened. Had he seen me perform? He had never been interested in my boarding. Thought it was stupid. I'd always wanted him to watch me, just once. But now that he was here, I wondered why. With Marc there was generally a reason that served him and no one else.

We made eye contact and he put his fingers in his mouth and whistled. It was a whistle that when we were young he had taught me to do. It had been our secret call.

CHAPTER FIVE

I jumped off the podium block and my heart was still racing. *Had* Marc seen my race? Marc always told me that I should be drumming and dancing or at least playing lacrosse.

With lanky strides, Marc approached me. He had a long lean build like my dad, while I was a bit shorter and stockier like my mom. I didn't want any of my friends to see me with him so I quickly scanned the crowd, and when I couldn't see Carrie or Allie my breath started to slow. They had said they would meet us inside for a hot chocolate when it was over. I blew out a gust of air.

"Good job, bro." He held up his fist.

"Thanks," I replied. I didn't fist him back.

"How much cash you win?"

My heart sank like a stone in the river. Of course that was why he was here. "Not much." I couldn't look him in the eye. "This isn't a big-enough event to win much. Some of the big events like X games or the U.S. Open have huge winnings." I had won $300, but I wasn't telling Marc that. He'd ask me to "front him a loan."

"I thought you won thousands at these things."

"Yeah, right," I said.

I had actually had a moment there when I thought that he'd *wanted* to watch me, that for once he was proud of me. How stupid was that? All he wanted was money. *My* money.

"Why don't you go in those big events then?" Marc asked. "You're good enough to win the big dough."

"I'm amateur," I snapped back.

He squinted and eyed my board before he looked back at me. "Heard you live in a nice pad."

My heart thudded to my toes. My throat dried and I tried to swallow before I said, "It's okay. Nothing great."

He winked at me. "Not what I heard." Then he patted my shoulder. "Well, congrats, little bro. Your big brother is proud of you."

He turned and walked away and I couldn't move. Not even an inch. How did he know where I lived? Did Dad tell him? Or did he weasel it out of Serena? I watched him go and that's when I saw the black truck waiting for him. He was with the same guys. The driver had this wild red hair and threw a cigarette butt out the window. He jerked his head in some nonverbal communication with Marc. The back door of the truck opened and Marc climbed in.

I jumped a foot, I swear, when I felt the tap on my shoulder.

"Great run, Jax," said Stu.

"Thanks." I tried to sound excited.

He frowned at me, just a little. "What's wrong?"

Of course he'd pick up on my mood. Stu could sense

the smallest problems in all of his athletes. It made him a great communicator. I faked a broad smile. "Nothing," I insisted. "It was a great day."

"I'll say. Go home and get rested for slope tomorrow."

Marc and I waded in the water with our fishing nets. The scorching-hot sun looked like a tangerine in the sky and it tanned our bare backs. Small fluffy white clouds dotted the horizon like cotton balls.

"I got one!" Marc yelled.

"How did you do that?" My voice squeaked.

Marc pushed his hands through the water to make his way over to me. "Like this, Jaxie," he said, guiding my hand through the water.

Within seconds I had a fish.

I woke up in a darkened room and sat up in bed. The red lights on my clock read 3:00 a.m. I groaned and flopped back on my pillow, thinking of that last summer with Marc. He and I had fished, skateboarded, played video games, and had basically done everything together all summer long until . . . he'd started coming home drunk and yelling at Dad because he hadn't brought us up on the reserve. The words still rang through my mind. "What kind of father are you to take away our roots? *Our heritage? To deprive of us of our culture?*"

His late-night accusations were like a broken record and I pressed my hands over my ears. I just couldn't make myself feel like Marc did. Sure, I liked visiting my grandparents and playing with my cousins who did live on the reserve, but I also always enjoyed getting in the car and driving back to the city. It was our home. One wasn't better than the other. They were both good.

The drinking started when Marc was thirteen.

The drugs at fifteen.

The knives at sixteen. I found the switchblade under his mattress one day when I was looking for a video game.

After that, I'd *really* started snowboarding, so I could get away from the house for the entire day and not listen to the fighting. I'd only been twelve.

I glanced at the clock and closed my eyes. I had to be up in five hours. The minutes ticked by and I tossed and turned. Every time I tried to visualize my slope run Marc's face popped into my mind, and another memory played like a movie reel.

The window lifted. I sat up in bed. Marc crawled through the window of the room we shared but didn't make it to his bed. Blood stained his clothes and matted his hair. He reeked of smoke and pot. I pushed off my covers, got out of bed, and crept to the door. Once I knew the hall was clear, I tiptoed to the bathroom. I wet some washcloths and brought them back to our room. I undressed Marc, got him into bed, and washed his face and hair. I tucked the duvet up to his chin. Softly, I sang to him. A Cree song my grandmother taught me.

I sighed. And looked at the clock. Again. Time was ticking by and I needed sleep. So many times I'd helped him. But then other times the cops brought him home. On those nights, I would sit by his bed and tell him to stop drinking and doing drugs and whatever else he was doing. Of course, he probably never heard me.

During that time in my life, Dad worked more.

Mom drank more.

I snowboarded more.

Serena, my little sister, read fantasy novels in her room.

Then my mom and dad split up.

Marc went with Mom. Our house got quiet and for the most part I liked it that way. Although in the silence, there were times I missed Marc for some stupid, crazy reason. I told myself over and over to forget about him. My mother, now, she was a different story. When she left, I sure didn't miss cleaning up her drunken mess.

No. I didn't want to think of her. If only I could sleep. I rocked in my bed, back and forth, to get rid of the old pictures, but they persisted.

I walked in, holding Serena's hand and kicked the shoes out of the way. Immediately I smelled sour milk.

"Pee-you," said Serena, holding her nose.

"Mom!" I called.

I heard the snores. "Wait here, Serena."

I walked into the living room. Passed out on the sofa, she looked pathetic. I glanced at the clock. Four hours until Dad came back to get us. I heard Serena's footsteps and turned.

"Is she sleeping?"

I nodded. "Let's go outside," I said. "I'll take you for french fries somewhere."

My eyes popped open. Serena. My little sister. When I was leaving for Podium, she sobbed and told me not to go. But today she had sounded good when I phoned. I had given her and Dad a quick call to tell them I had won my contest, but I hadn't mentioned that Marc was in Calgary. Not sure why. Was I still trying to protect him? I was sure no one in my family knew he was here. Not even my mother, with whom he still sort of lived — when he needed a bed for a night.

For another few hours, I tossed and turned. I guess I must have fallen asleep at some point, maybe around six, because I awoke from a deep sleep when my alarm went off at eight. I dragged my weary body to the bathroom and wondered how I was going to get through the day. If only I had until noon to sleep.

Snow fell from a dull grey sky and I scraped my windows before I jumped in my car. I cranked up Blake Shelton and drove to the hill. After signing in at the tent and putting clean Burton stickers on my board, I made my way to the lift. My body felt tired and achy. I had to get warmed up, get rid of the kinks in my joints.

My practice run sucked and I almost bit it huge as I tried what normally was an easy rail ride. The muscles in my legs quivered and my balance was a bit off.

At the bottom of the hill, I saw Rob and he waved. I waved back but made my way right back to the chairlift, instead of hiking up. Once I got to the top, I slid off the chair and sat down in the snow to fasten my board. I looked up into the wispy falling snow. Soft snowflakes landed on my face and quickly turned into cold water. I shook my head and placed my goggles over my eyes. This was just one day. And I could do it without sleep. I didn't have to perform tomorrow so I could go all out today. Tonight I would get rest. With that thought planted in my mind, I stood up and stared down the hill. Forget about Marc and my lack of sleep and perform to my best ability. This is who I was: a snowboarder. I couldn't let Marc take that away from me.

After a few more runs, I lined up at the top for my turn to drop. Half pipe was my specialty, but slope came in a close second. And I had a good run planned. Stu and I had worked it out over the past few months and he'd encouraged me to try a few new daring moves — like a 450 off the close-out rail.

They announced my name and I mentally focused on what was in front of me. Forget the judges, forget Marc, and just do what I did best. I sucked in a deep breath and as I was blowing out the air, I dropped. Adrenalin surged through me. Every instinct told me to slow down, but with every rail, I went for massive air. At the height of my 270 out of the down rail, while in mid-air, I decided to add something extra to my turn. My body spun, and I was on that edge of being out of control, but I also had this unbelievable momentum. It felt amazing. One wrong movement and I could lose it completely. All the right movements and I would have a spectacular run!

I landed, squeezed my thigh muscles, and cruised across the finish line. I grinned. I had just performed the best run of my life.

When I was out of my board and on the other side of the fence, Stu approached me. "Jax, that was spectacular. I think you may have just broken through a personal barrier."

"Thanks." I couldn't stop grinning.

He tilted his head and squinted. "What made you switch up mid-air?"

"I had such good height. I didn't really think about it. I just did it."

"That takes guts. And confidence in your technical abilities."

"Or craziness," I added, laughing.

He patted my shoulder. "In this sport you have to take risks to make it big. You just did that."

At the end of the day, I stood on the podium to receive my second gold medal of the weekend. When I faced the crowd I didn't see Marc, and something pinched me inside. Disappointment maybe. I wanted him to see what I had accomplished. But then relief washed over me. Maybe he had gone back to Montreal.

Before I drove home, I sat in my car in the parking lot and called my dad.

"I won again," I said. I scraped the side window with my fingernail. My car took so long to heat up.

"Way to go, Jax!" A true supporter, my dad, and his enthusiastic comment made me smile.

"Best run of my life," I continued. The tiredness I had felt in the morning hadn't followed me through the day and now I was buzzing.

"Well," said my dad, "this school has been good for you."

"Is Serena there?" I asked. "I want to tell her."

"She's out with a friend."

"Who?" I sat up a little. Lately she'd been hanging out with a couple of kids I thought were bad news.

"Kelsey."

I relaxed. "That's okay," I said.

My dad laughed. "Stop worrying. She's got a good head on her shoulders."

"So did Marc," I whispered. As soon as his name was out of my mouth I regretted it.

"Have you heard from him?" Dad asked. His voice sounded strange. Yes, he had kicked Marc out, but he still kept tabs on him. Did he know he was in Calgary? I didn't want to worry Dad if Marc had gone back to Montreal. Anyway, I knew Marc was in Calgary for no good reason, and Dad would start worrying. The stress would make his blood pressure go up.

"I talked to him the other day," I said, trying to choose my words carefully.

"Did he call you?"

"Yeah," I lied. Well, sort of lied. He *had* phoned. I never lied to my dad, not after seeing how Marc concocted so many stories over the years.

"My gut tells me something is wrong." Dad's words were almost a whisper.

"Why do you say that?" I asked. "He's disappeared before, Dad. For days."

"I know." He sighed. "It's just a feeling."

"Well, tell Serena to call me later," I said.

"Sure thing. And, Jax, I'm really proud of you."

CHAPTER SIX

"Pizza's ready!" Mrs. Marino yelled from the top of the stairs.

"I'm starving." Rob hurdled the sofa. "Coming!" He ran up the stairs, Kade, Nathan, Quinn, and Aaron right behind him.

I took Carrie's hand and pulled her up. "Come on, let's eat."

"Let's watch a scary movie after dinner," said Allie, moving her shoulders up and down as if she was dancing to her words. She walked ahead of us with Sophia and Parm.

"Yeah, let's." Carrie's eyes lit up. "I love scary movies."

"The food smells so good!" Allie put her nose in the air and sniffed. Then she turned and grinned. "Last one there has to do dishes." She took the stairs three at a time, and her long legs made it look easy. The other girls followed but not as quickly. I trailed because I would do dishes anyway — it was my billet house.

The island countertop was covered with food. Square pieces of pepperoni pizza sizzled on big round plates, and a heaping dish of chicken wings sat to one side of the island.

On the other side a big wooden bowl overflowed with homemade Caesar salad. The tantalizing smells lingered in the kitchen. Mrs. Marino had also put out containers of orange juice and milk.

"There are two types of wings," said Mrs. Marino. "Hot and teriyaki. And I figured you kids needed some greens, so I made a big salad. And I only made pepperoni pizza. That's all Rob and Jax eat."

"Paper plates." Allie picked up one and waved it in my face as she hip-checked me. "You're out of doing the dishes even though you were last up the stairs."

I had just finished piling salad on my plate when Daniel, my billet brother, walked into the kitchen dressed in his soccer gear, followed by Mr. Marino. He was home from his business trip and was casually dressed in jeans and a pullover. For work he wore dark suits, crisp white shirts, and expensive ties.

When she saw them, Mrs. Marino quickly took off her apron. "I'd better get ready."

Daniel glanced at the clock. "Mom, we have to leave in three minutes."

"We'll clean up," piped up Rob from the table.

I turned to Daniel. "Hey, Dan, good luck tonight, eh?"

"Thanks," he said seriously. "The team we're playing is tied with us for first."

I held up my hand and he fisted me. "Let me know when your next game is," I said. "I want to come watch. Last time I was there you scored two goals." I glanced over at Mr. Marino. "We'll take care of putting everything away," I said.

He nodded his head and smiled. "I know you will."

Mrs. Marino was ready in less than three minutes and then she and Mr. Marino left to take Daniel to his game.

Everyone was hungry and ate so fast that we were finished chowing down and cleaning up in forty minutes flat.

Carrie wiped the counter one last time and folded the dish rag, hanging it on the bar in front of the sink.

"Looks spotless," said Allie. "Come on, everyone. Scary movie time."

"I hate scary movies," said Kade. "They freak me out."

"So," said Allie, "hide under the covers."

We all went back downstairs and Allie got the movie organized. Rob got a bunch of blankets and everyone found a spot to hang out.

At the first big scary part the girls screamed, well, everyone but Parm.

"It's so fake," she said. "I watched this documentary once and they showed all the tricks they use to make it look real." Parm was probably the smartest girl at Podium. I couldn't figure out how her brain did what it did.

"Shh," said Carrie. "Don't wreck it for us."

Nathan laughed. "This is so stupid."

"Oh no! Now he's going after her friend!" Sophia shrieked and covered her eyes again. Then Nathan and Quinn screamed just to be funny before they started wrestling on the floor. Soon, Aaron and Kade were wrestling too.

"Hey," yelled Parm over the noise. "I think I hear the doorbell."

"I'll get it," I said. "Probably a neighbour kid wanting bottles for a bottle drive."

I ran up the stairs, opened the door with a speech all ready to tell the kids to come back later, and instead saw three guys on the doorstep. I immediately recognized the red-haired guy who, just yesterday, had been driving the truck my brother got into. One other guy was blond, and one was First Nations. What were they doing here? My pulse quickened. Cold washed over me.

I didn't see Marc.

"Heard there's a party going on here," the blond guy said, his words slurred. He was obviously drunk. My body stiffened and my hands automatically curled into fists. This wasn't good. Not good at all. Instead of having the flight or fright response, I tensed, ready to fight. Which made no sense. Three guys to one; what was I thinking?

"No," I replied. "You got the wrong house."

The red-haired guy smirked. His pupils were huge. I sucked in some air. Drunk *and* high: a really bad combo. I peered up and over their heads, looking for Marc, but I couldn't see him.

"I don't think so," said the redhead, who had now moved a step closer to me. "This is the address we were given."

"Yeah, right. By who?"

"Your brother, kid."

"Where is he then? I don't see him."

The guy pulled out a switchblade, snapped it open, and touched the blade with his fingertip. "I'm not sure." He ran it along his face as he sneered at me.

"Well, there's no party here," I said firmly, hoping they couldn't hear the tremor in my voice. Again, I glanced over their shoulders to see if Marc was somewhere in the distance. Was he back at the truck? Standing on the side-walk? Hiding in the bushes? My blood raced and my heart was beating out of control.

Or . . . had they done something to him?

Rob appeared to stand beside me. "What's going on?" he asked.

"Nothing. Go back downstairs. I can handle this."

"We're coming in." The redhead put a foot on the door-step.

"Guys! We need help!" Rob yelled toward the stairs.

I tried to close the door, but the red-haired guy pushed it with his hand. I pushed back with both hands. Rob joined me, and we leaned against the door, using our body weight to keep them out.

"Keep pushing, Jax!" Rob used his shoulder.

"Hey, what's going on up here?" Aaron asked. Nathan, Quinn, and Kade were all upstairs now and in the front hallway.

"These guys are trying to come in the house!" This time Rob really laid his shoulder into the door. He turned and whispered, "They've got knives."

"Knives?" Aaron's eyes widened. "Are you serious? We need to call the cops." He pulled out his phone and di-alled.

"We can hold them off until they get here." Nathan balled his hands into fists and stood tall. He was known as a scrappy lacrosse player.

"We need something to hit them with," said Quinn, his words coming out fast. "I bet there's some hockey sticks in the garage."

Suddenly the pressure on the door was gone, making Rob and I almost lose our footing. Footsteps could be heard retreating down the outside stairs. Rob and I looked at each other. Aaron pressed END on his phone.

"Are they leaving?" Rob whispered.

"Or maybe they just went around the back," Kade said.

Nathan ran to the front window and peered out through the wooden slats on the blinds. "They're heading back to the truck," he said.

"Can you see the license plate?" Aaron asked.

"Way too far away," answered Nathan. "I'm not even sure if the truck is black or blue or what kind it is. So hard to see."

"I could run outside and try to get the number," said Aaron. "I'm quick."

"We must have scared them," said Quinn.

I narrowed my eyes. I couldn't believe it was this easy. And deep down I knew it wasn't over yet. Sweat beaded on my forehead. My throat was totally parched. I tried to catch my breath as I walked over to the window to stand beside Nathan and look through the blinds. The guys were definitely at the truck and seemed to be getting inside, and I still didn't see Marc. He must have told them where I lived. None of this made any sense. If he did tell them then where was he?

"Too late to get info on the truck," said Nathan. "They're in it now and it's driving away."

"Probably going to another party somewhere," said Kade. He snapped his fingers. "I heard that Carly chick was having a party tonight. We should phone and warn her." Kade pulled his cell out of the top pocket of his shirt and found her number.

"Hey, just a heads-up," he said into the phone. "There's a gang of guys driving around looking for parties to crash. They're bad news."

"Tell her one has red hair, one's blond, and one's First Nations," said Rob loudly. He looked at everyone. "They could be part of an inner-city gang of some sort."

Yes, *one guy* was First Nations. But he wasn't Marc. Only I knew the Marinos' house had been targeted because of my brother. Did they just want to scare us? Was that it? Had Marc done something to make them mad and now they were coming to me for payback? Did he owe them money?

The questions piled up in my brain and I had no answers to any of them. Why would they back off so easily? They had made the trip out here for some reason. And they were leaving without getting anything. Maybe they didn't realize there'd be so many guys here.

"Who do you think those guys were?" Allie's voice trembled and she had her arms crossed over her chest. All the girls were now upstairs too and they looked scared. None of them had said anything because Quinn had warned them to stay quiet.

"I don't know." I shook my head, hoping no one could tell I was lying.

"Something about the red-haired guy is familiar," said Rob. He frowned as if he was thinking hard.

"I've never seen them before." I hated lying but I had to. No one could find out that in the past few days I'd seen that truck twice, and both times my brother had been with those guys. Rob could have seen it the day my brother talked to him in the parking lot at the hill.

"I'm positive I've seen that guy before." Rob frowned as if trying to put two and two together.

"I don't think so, dude," I said. "It's just random."

"Maybe we should all go home," said Sophia. She sounded way more scared now than when she was watching the movie. Her voice quivered and she had her arms wrapped around her body.

I put my hand to my forehead and closed my eyes. I was still shaking too. Maybe everyone *should* leave.

"I agree," said Rob. "They probably thought there was a party here because of the cars. There are guys like them who just go around rich neighbourhoods looking for tons of cars so they can wreck parties. I've heard of a few gangs coming out this way. It happened last year. It takes so long for the cops to show up out here that they know they can get away with trashing parties and stealing things. They probably won't come back. Let's hope they don't anyway."

"Should we still call the police?" Sophia asked.

"I think we should," said Parm. "Those guys didn't take or wreck anything, and I'm not sure the cops would come out, but it doesn't hurt to let them know in case the creeps are looking for another place to hit."

"Parm's right," said Allie.

"I'll make the call," said Rob.

"I'm gonna get my coat," said Sophia. "Who's coming with me?"

"Me," said Allie, raising her hand.

Within seconds everyone had their coats on and those driving were impatiently jingling their keys.

"I hope you guys will be okay," said Carrie to me and

Rob. "You can come home with me if you want."

"We'll be fine," I replied. "The Marinos will be home in less than an hour. We'll lock all the doors."

CHAPTER SEVEN

After everyone had left, the house took on an eerie silence. Rob and I looked at each other. He immediately went to the door and locked it, the sound of the latch catching echoing in the quiet house.

"That was so weird," he said.

I exhaled and ran my hand through my hair. "At least nothing was broken or taken."

"Yeah, for sure," said Rob. "I don't think my heart has ever beat so fast before."

I exhaled loudly and rubbed my temples with my fingers. "I'm with you," I said. "My head feels like it'll explode."

"The whole thing just seems so random." Rob shook his head.

"I'm going downstairs," I said.

My brother was involved somehow, but I couldn't tell Rob that. But where *was* Marc? I had to phone home and let Dad know that he was here and in some kind of trouble. "I gotta call my dad," I mumbled.

"I'm gonna make that call to the cops," said Rob. He patted his pockets. "My phone's downstairs." He snapped his fingers. "Shoot," he said. "We should've taken a photo to show the cops. That would've been great evidence."

We were halfway down the stairs when suddenly the air was punctuated with a huge crash. The sound of shattering glass pierced the air. Someone had broken a window.

"What the heck!" Rob yelled. "Now I'm really calling the cops. They're back!" Rob flew downstairs to get his phone.

"Sounds like they broke a window in the garage," I yelled. "You call the cops and I'll go lock the garage door."

I took the stairs two at a time and ran through the kitchen to the door that led to the garage. The Marinos would have left through the garage, so the door wouldn't be locked.

Another splintering crash punctuated the air. This time the noise came from the back of the house.

I could hear Rob frantically talking on the phone to the police dispatcher. The cops would be here soon. We had to hold these guys off until they got here. By now I was at the door that led to the garage. I turned the knob and, sure enough, the door leading from the house to the garage was not locked.

Then I heard movement. In the garage. I held my breath. The intruders couldn't hear me. I was about to click the lock on the door when I heard the voice. "I knew the boards would be in here."

It was Marc!

He was stealing my snowboards! Adrenalin rushed through me. There was no way I'd let anyone steal my boards. Without thinking of who was in the garage with him, I flung open the door and flipped on the lights. I quickly glanced around, and when I saw it was just him, I jumped down the three steps and ran toward him.

"Marc, what are you doing? Don't take our boards!"

"They're worth big bucks, little bro," he said. His words were slurred,

"They're mine! And Rob's!"

"So?" He turned to me and that's when I saw his dilated pupils. I ground to a halt. When Marc was high and drunk, confronting him was a mistake. He could get violent and take a few punches. Those guys earlier had knives. Did Marc too? Perhaps I could talk him down. I used to be able to, now and again. How much time did I have before the other guys showed up?

Where were they? I hoped Rob was okay in the house.

Marc looked at me with glazed eyes. "Come on, little bro. You know that if I take 'em you'll just get more. You're the guy who wins big all the time. Stands on the podium like a big-shot athlete. Professional athletes make huge dough. That's you, little bro."

He was babbling, just like he used to when we was on meth.

Noise sounded from the other side of the door to the house. Marc picked up a board, ready for action. I also glanced around for something like a baseball bat or hockey stick. I'd lost my chance to talk him down. My heart sped up again. Who was coming?

"Jax!" screamed Rob, flinging open the door. "They're taking stuff from the house. You've gotta help me. They've got the TV and they're in Mrs. Marino's . . ."

He stopped screeching and stared at Marc. Then it was like a surge of electricity zapped him.

"Hey, that's my board!" Rob literally leaped off the stair landing, missing all the steps. He landed on the garage floor and hurled himself at Marc.

I tried to reach out to stop him but he dodged me. Marc reacted faster than I thought he was capable of in his drugged state. He spun around with the board in his hands and whacked Rob.

The thud echoed off the garage walls. Rob's head snapped back. His body caved and he dropped like lead to the cold cement floor. Blood seeped from his head.

His body looked lifeless.

"What have you done?!" I screamed at Marc as I fell to my knees beside Rob and gently shook his shoulders.

"Come on, buddy, get up." My heart ticked like a bomb. This was bad. Really bad. "He's totally out of it. Marc, you've knocked him out!" I slapped Rob's cheeks, again very gently, but his eyes remained closed.

"He shouldn't have come at me." Marc's voice quivered.

I glared up at him. "What is wrong with you? Why would you do something like this?" I jumped up and pushed him. "Get out of here."

He didn't push me back. I pushed him again. "You wreck everything. You wrecked our family and now you've come here to wreck my life. Why couldn't you just stay home?" I shouted at Marc and it shocked me. I never shouted at him.

His shoulders slumped and his dark eyes filled with hurt. It was as if I'd sucker-punched him. I had to look away.

"I'm sorry," he mumbled. "I'm a screw-up."

Sirens sounded in the distance.

"Did you call the cops?" he asked, his voice a whisper. "Shit, shit, shit. I can't go to jail. I just can't. Is he alive? Is he alive? Jax, make him wake up."

I bent over Rob again. "Wake up. Come on, wake up. Please, dude. Come on. You can do it."

"The cops catch me for this, I'll go to prison," Marc said. "You gotta help me, little bro. I'm on probation. You *gotta* help me. Damnit. Shit."

Marc's pleading was like a jab in the stomach. I glanced up at him. Pathetic. He looked so pathetic. His eyes were wide and filled with terror and despair. His lips were a thin line, stretched across his face. His cheeks were sunken and hollow-looking.

I wanted to cave. Tell him I was sorry. Instead I said, "Tell someone who cares."

The siren wailed, closer and closer. Then we must have both heard the same sound at the same time, because we both turned our ears to the garage door. On the other side of the door was the sound of tires squealing and a truck rumbling and speeding down the road.

"Open the door! Let me out of here. I have to catch them."

"The switch is on the side wall," I said. I wasn't leaving Rob's side.

Marc ran for the switch, flipped it, and the garage door squealed open. Snow drifted in.

"They left me." Marc visibly trembled in the cold draft and he wrapped his scrawny arms around his body. "What am I gonna do?" He started pacing and slapping his gloved hands together and the repetitive sound seemed to blast through my brain. Almost as if every clap was a gunshot.

"Just go!" I shouted. "Get out of here. Go through the back door. *Now.*"

"You got my back, right, Jaxie?" Marc sounded like a whining dog. "You got my back. Just like you always did."

"Go."

"Jaxie, you're the best brother a guy could have."

He took off out the back door of the garage with only minutes to get away. And I let him go.

CHAPTER EIGHT

The police and ambulance arrived, red lights flashing, lighting the black sky. Snow fell, big chunks of wet fluff. Rob had wanted me to go to Lake Louise tomorrow and cruise through powder. He loved fresh snow. Because I couldn't go, he had made plans to go with another friend.

I talked to him. Lowered my head to his and talked in his ear. "You're going to Lake Louise tomorrow. To catch some powder," I whispered. "It'll be so deep in the trees."

Marc was long gone; out the back door of the garage and to the streets. I wondered if the snow would cover his tracks. Maybe his friends picked him up a few streets over. Or he was on the highway, heading out to the Morley reserve — he had friends there, I figured, though I didn't know. I didn't care. I stayed huddled over Rob, holding his hand, talking to him. Every few seconds his body convulsed, making me believe he was going to open his eyes, but they stayed shut.

"We'll take it from here," said a paramedic.

"Were you the one who made the call?" a policeman asked. Two had shown up, a male and a female. I got to my feet.

"No," I replied. "He did." I pointed to Rob. "From his cell."

The paramedics slipped a stretcher underneath Rob and strapped him on. I watched, unable to make direct eye contact with the police.

Rob still hadn't gained consciousness. "You're going to be okay," I said as they started to cart him away.

"I'd like to ask you a few routine questions." The male cop spoke with zero expression in his voice.

I shoved my hands in the pockets of my jeans, suddenly realizing that I was outside without a coat or mitts and I was now alone with two cops. And a truly horrible situation.

I rubbed my forehead and nodded.

"Perhaps we should go into the house," said the female cop.

"Okay," I said.

I led the two cops into the house and to the kitchen.

"The people we live with aren't home," I said. "They will be soon. I think we should call them."

"So, this isn't your house?" The male cop glanced around the kitchen.

"No," I answered. "I go to Podium Sports Academy and Rob and I billet here. I'm from Montreal. Rob's from Rossland."

"What happened here tonight?"

I proceeded to tell the story, leaving out the details of my brother's involvement. Just as I finished, the female cop tilted her head for a second, then got up and walked toward the window in the living room. "Sounds as if the people you live with just drove up."

The male cop quickly glanced at her. "Go talk to them. I want to ask this young man a few more routine questions."

The female officer headed to the front door. I heard it open and shut before a weird silence took over the room. Almost like a freaky hush. I felt alone and trapped and suddenly really, really scared. This cop had mean-looking eyes and he stared at me with disdain. I'd seen this look before when I was a little kid in grade school and a big kid had decided to take a dislike to me because I was First Nations. I tried to hold on to my composure and not let him see me trembling.

"I'd like you to tell me one more time what happened tonight." The cop's demeanour really had changed. Gone was his neutral tone and in its place was something that, to me, sounded accusatory.

"A bunch of guys just showed up at the door." I tried to say exactly the same thing I'd said the first time. "They wanted in and we said no. There were ten of us here then. That's all Mrs. Marino wanted us to have over." I stopped to catch my breath. My heart beat wildly underneath my clothes. The cop had already asked me for the names and numbers of all my friends, which I'd given readily. I needed to add we weren't drinking or doing anything wrong. He had to know that.

I started talking again. "We were just having a get-together and Mrs. Marino had made pizza and wings." Why was I talking about what food we had to eat? "Rob and I had just been in a snowboarding contest at Winsport." I stopped again. Just to breathe and think, knowing that my mind was going in a million directions and I wasn't following the script like I'd planned.

"Continue," said the cop.

I met his unflinching gaze when I said, "We weren't drinking or anything."

The comment didn't change the disdainful expression on his face as I was hoping it would. We First Nations got a bad rep because everyone thought we were a bunch of drunks. I wasn't. My dad wasn't. And my white mother *was*. Go figure.

"What happened with the men who showed up at the door?" he asked as if I hadn't already told him.

I ran my hands up and down my jeans, staring at my fingernails as they scratched the denim. "They said they heard there was a party. They must have seen the cars." I stopped moving my hands and glanced toward the living room for a second. I kept hoping the front door would open soon.

I turned my attention back to the cop and tried to look him in the eye, but it was so hard to hold his gaze. He had this cold hard stare that seemed to go through my skin and right to my nerves. I shivered but I continued, "Then they left and we thought they wouldn't come back. Everyone went home but Rob and me because we live here. We didn't think they'd come back but they did."

"How did your friend get hurt?"

I shrugged and glanced away for a second. "I don't know," I said. "The second time they came back they were running around outside breaking windows, and then they came inside and started to take things from the house."

"You didn't answer my question."

"He must have got hit with a snowboard."

The policeman casually leaned back, and if he'd had a toothpick I bet he would have picked his teeth. He lifted one eyebrow. "How do you know that?"

My hands trembled and I clenched them in my lap. Had I just made a huge error? "It was, uh, it was lying on the floor. Rob would never leave his board on the floor like that." I shrugged again. "I guess I just assumed," I muttered. This was not going well.

The cop nodded, slowly, and the gesture made me break out in a sweat. I kept glancing at the door. Where were the Marinos? Why didn't they come and save me from this questioning? The female cop had gone outside ages ago. If they were home they should have been in the house by now.

"So you didn't actually see who hit him with the board?"

I shook my head. No words came out of my mouth.

"What did they take?" the cop asked, changing the subject.

My throat constricted. Was this another trick question? I hadn't really seen them take anything. I remembered Rob yelling at me. "Just stuff. A television, I think."

"You don't know what for sure?"

"No. It was just so crazy. We were, uh, we were just running around trying to figure out what to do. Rob yelled to me that they were taking a television. He also said they were in Mrs. Marino's room."

"Okay. Let's get back to your friend."

Rob. I closed my eyes for a second and tried to breathe normally. Rob was in an ambulance right now, on his way to the hospital. "I hope he's going to be okay," I mumbled.

"Me too, kid, me too." The cop's eyes softened. He did have a heart. Maybe he had children.

But within seconds he stared me down again with his steely gaze. "Did you see anyone? Can you give us any description of the guys?"

"One guy had red hair," I said. "He was the one at the door the first time they came here. And he wore a headband. And there was another guy with blond hair and one with darker hair too."

"Would you say the darker-haired guy was like you, *native?*"

I didn't like how he said that and it made me shake. I hated being labelled. "Yeah," I said. "He was native."

"But you don't know him?"

"No," I said. "I'd never seen him before."

"And there were just three?"

"Yes." Did he somehow know Marc was here too?

He tapped his pen. The noise bounced off the walls. I bit my lower lip. There was no way I would break down in front of this guy.

"You said they came in a vehicle. Can you describe it?"

Maybe if I said what the truck looked like I could steer the cops away from Marc. It wasn't his truck. Maybe they would pin everything on those other guys. "It was a black truck," I stated.

"Not blue or maybe black but definitely black?"

The way he asked this made me wonder if I'd stepped on a land mine. "Yes," I replied.

"Could you give me the make of the truck?"

"Ford," I answered without hesitation.

He tilted his head. "You could see the colour *and* what kind of vehicle it was in the pitch black? You must have incredible eyesight. Did they drive it up the driveway? Is that how you were able to see all these little details?"

"Um, my . . . my dad used to have one exactly like it." I stumbled over my words. "And I saw it from the window, but they didn't come up the driveway."

He slowly nodded his head, only once. "So . . . you didn't know any of the guys at all? Never seen them before?"

I shook my head.

"You know kid, I wish I could believe you but something isn't adding up for me. You *people* think you can do whatever you want and get away with it." He leaned closer to me. "You're given way too much. Why do I have to pay for my daughter's education and you get it for free? And here's a little story for you. A kid just like you killed my cousin up north on the rigs. You can't get away with everything. We'll catch them." He smiled and not a nice smile. "*All* of them. And that means you."

I wanted to hold his gaze, but I was trembling and felt sick to my stomach, so I glanced down at my feet.

Just then the front door opened and relief washed over me. Mrs. Marino rushed over and hugged me. "Are you okay?"

"Did they take anything from my room?" Daniel asked.

"I don't know, Dan." I looked at Mrs. Marino. "I'm okay. But Rob's not. He got hit with a snowboard." My voice cracked.

I looked over at Mr. Marino. "I'm so sorry. I have no

idea what they took. I think a television, but I don't know what else."

"I'll call our insurance company," he said, putting his hand on my shoulder. "Jax, it's just stuff. We are more concerned about Rob right now than anything else."

"We thought they'd gone the first time," I babbled. "I want to go to the hospital to see Rob. He wasn't awake when they took him away."

Mrs. Marino looked from the male cop to the female cop. "Do you need to ask him any more questions?"

The male cop eyed me before he smiled and said, "No. He's free to go." Then he added, "For now. I'll leave my card." He handed me his business card. "If you think of anything else, give me a call."

The cop turned to Mr. Marino. "We'd like permission to go through the house to assess the damage. And check the garage and also out back, if that's okay with you. And since it is a crime scene, we will seal off the garage so the Crime Scene Unit will be able to do their job properly. They're on their way now and they'll be checking for fingerprints, so please don't touch anything. It would be best to leave your cars outside."

"Absolutely," said Mr. Marino.

The police and Mr. Marino left the kitchen, with Daniel on their heels. When they were out of sight, my shoulders sagged. How could Marc have gotten me into this? I had just lied to the police. What would happen to me if they found out I had lied? Would I go to jail too?

Mrs. Marino broke into my whirling thoughts. "Jax, it's not your fault."

"Rob got hit pretty hard. I-I, uh, have to go see him."

"Are you sure you're okay to drive?" Mrs. Marino asked. "This is just awful what happened to you boys. But the police will find out who did it."

"Yeah, I'm fine to drive," I answered quickly.

Only I wasn't fine. I wasn't fine at all. I had to see Rob to make sure he was okay.

Within minutes I was outside and had brushed the snow off my car with the sleeve of my jacket. The police cruiser still sat in the driveway. The garage had been cordoned off with yellow tape and I could hear voices in the backyard, so I got in my car ASAP, and even though it wasn't close to being warmed up, I shoved it in reverse.

About halfway to the hospital my phone rang. What if it was Marc? I made a sharp turn and pulled over to the side. It wasn't Marc though.

"Hey, Carrie," I said.

"How are you?" she asked. "I was worried about you guys. We shouldn't have left you."

I thought about lying and not telling her about Rob, but I'd already lied to the police. "Rob is in the hospital," I said.

"What?" She almost shrieked on the phone. "What happened?"

"Long story," I said. "They came back then some guy hit him with a snowboard in the garage." I leaned back and looked at the fraying fabric in the roof of my car. What would happen if I pulled that one hanging thread? Would it all unravel?

My lies going were going to end up unravelling too. Rob had seen my brother. And I had lied to the police about Marc being there. Maybe, just maybe, I'd given Marc time to get away. If Rob was okay, and he had to be okay, maybe Marc wouldn't get charged with anything. I put my forehead on the steering wheel. My mind was going in too many directions.

"Were they the guys who were at the house earlier? Omigod, this is horrible. Are you okay?" Carrie asked.

"Yeah." I sat up and looked forward again at the snowy road. I flipped on my windshield wipers.

"This is so awful," she said. "Where are you now?"

"On my way to the hospital."

"I'll meet you there."

Something inside me bristled. I didn't want to have to make small talk with Carrie or talk through this with her. I wanted to be alone. "Have you talked to the police yet?" I asked.

"No. Why do you ask *that?*"

"I had to give everyone's name to them. They will probably call." I didn't want Carrie to see me. What if she read something in my face, my eyes? She had this uncanny sense and could pick up on things. She always knew when something was wrong. "Are you sure you want to drive in the snow?" I blurted out.

Silence on the other end. After a few seconds she spoke. "Why would you ask me that? Of course, I would drive in the snow to see a friend who's in the hospital. And to see you. You've been through something horrible too."

"I, uh, just thought it was kind of late," I said.

"I'm coming Jax."

I sighed. "Drive carefully, okay?"

CHAPTER NINE

Rob was in the Intensive Care Unit at the Foothills hospital in Calgary. At first the nurses didn't want me to go in to see him, but luckily Coach Stu showed up and he convinced the nurses that I should be put on the friends and family list. I didn't wait for Carrie.

"Did they tell you anything?" I asked Stu as we washed our hands at a disinfectant container on the wall just before the set of double doors that led to the ICU.

"No. They're monitoring his brain very closely. They've probably put a shunt in it to stop it from swelling. It's critical they keep the swelling down."

"Swelling?" I walked beside Stu through the doors and into a part of the hospital I had never been before. There were rows of beds separated by white curtains. Machines hummed beside the beds and nurses moved constantly. Every patient seemed unconscious or severely injured. Some were bandaged, many attached to machines. The few that had their eyes open stared into space.

"The brain is very sensitive," said Stu. "He must have taken a hard blow."

The thud of the board hitting his head echoed in my brain.

"I called his parents," said Stu. "They're on their way. I hate to see them driving when it's snowing, but they insisted. They said they would leave right away and drive all night. They'll be here in the early morning. They said it was better than waiting for a flight."

"I've met them," I said. "They're so nice."

We rounded a corner and Stu said, "There he is."

I stopped walking. I couldn't move. Hooked up to an oxygen machine and an IV machine, wearing head gear and a neck brace, Rob lay very still on the bed. His eyes were closed and the only thing that moved was his chest going up and down.

I swear my heart froze in my chest. I didn't want to go to his bedside. This was eerie, like a bad movie. But way worse. The movie we had watched earlier in the evening had been fake and stupid, and this one was real.

"The first twenty-four hours are crucial," said Stu. He moved to Rob's bedside and bent down, getting closer to his ear. "Hey, Rob, it's Coach Stu. Jax and I are here to see you. You're going to get better and be back on your board in no time."

Stu looked at me and motioned for me to come closer.

A tennis ball seemed to have lodged in my throat. I tried to swallow but couldn't, and I could hardly get any air into my lungs. I inched forward to stand beside the bed on the opposite side of Stu.

Stu glanced over at me. "They say if you talk to people when they're unconscious they might be able to hear."

I took a deep breath and looked down at Rob. "Hey," was all I said. My voice cracked. I didn't know what else to say. This was so strange for me.

"Keep going," encouraged Stu.

"You're going to get better," I said softly, "and we're going to go to Lake Louise and hit some big powder." I took his hand in mine. It felt limp.

The machines continued to hum and buzz in the background. I squeezed his fingers. He didn't squeeze back. "You have to wake up, dude."

Stu touched my arm. "I'm going to leave you alone with him for a few minutes," he said. "Just keep talking to him."

After Stu left, I squeezed Rob's hand again. "I'm so sorry," I whispered. "This is my fault." I swiped at my eyes.

Why had I tried to protect Marc?

What was wrong with me?

My friend was comatose in the ICU and I was protecting the person who put him there. I leaned forward. "You're going to pull through this," I said. "And I will do the right thing by you."

The nurse came in a few seconds later and walked over to the side of the bed. She yelled in Rob's ear. "Rob, can you hear me?"

His fingers twitched.

She looked over at me and said, "I'm trying to see if he'll react."

"I thought I felt his hand move," I said.

"That's good. Seeing and feeling movement is important to his recovery." Next she pried open one of his eyes and shone light into it with a skinny flashlight. She moved the light back and forth across his eye.

"What's that for?" I asked.

She flicked off the flashlight. "I want to see if his eye will track, follow the light. If it does, it's a really good sign his brain is functioning in some capacity. Now I'm going to pull the curtains and see if he needs changing. Did you want to stay for that?"

"I'll go," I said. I squeezed Rob's hand one more time before I left.

Carrie met me in the lobby and gave me a huge long hug, and I have to admit it did feel good. I held her close and rested my cheek on the top of her head. "He's still not awake," I whispered.

She pulled back and touched my cheek. "What a horrible night for you."

"Worse for Rob," I muttered.

Carrie frowned. "Why do people have to do stuff like that?" She shook her head. "Why do they want to hurt other people? What did Rob ever do to anyone but make them laugh?"

"Alcohol and drugs change people." I looked down at the tiled floor. "Make them do stupid things."

"This is beyond stupid. You were right. The police called and asked questions. I said I didn't see the guys, but that they did come to the house and try to get in."

"I'm sure they'll talk to everyone," I said.

"I hope they catch the guys. Especially the one who did this to Rob. This is like attempted murder."

I wanted to say, "Me too," but the guy they had to catch was my brother. What if they did catch Marc? Then what?

Marc would go to jail and Dad would have to pay to bail him out with money he didn't have, money that could be used to help Serena be successful in some way. Marc was over eighteen and he had previous priors. This could definitely be attempted murder for him.

"Hey." Carrie touched my cheek again. "You want to get a coffee or something?"

"Sure," I said. "After I make a few phone calls."

"There's a late-night cafeteria open. You make your calls and I'll be right back."

The first call I made was to the Marinos to tell them I was staying at the hospital all night. If I had to, I would sleep in a chair. Yes, Mrs. Marino was worried about me, I could tell, but I convinced her I would be okay. She said she trusted me. That made my heart fall to my toes. Once she found out I'd lied to everyone, she wouldn't feel that way about me ever again. No one would. She had talked to Rob's parents and they would be arriving around four in the morning. I told her I wanted to be here for Rob until they arrived. She agreed and with a warm sound to her voice, said I was a good friend.

Some friend.

The next call I wanted to make was to Dad. It was later in Montreal, past midnight. What would I say to him? That Marc hit my friend with a snowboard when he was high and drunk, and now my friend was fighting for his life in the hospital? That I had let Marc run away so he didn't have to suffer any consequences? Earlier in the week I had lied to Dad and not even told him Marc was in Calgary. So I had to think of how to tell Dad. He had been hurt so many times by Marc and I knew this one might take him over his limit.

The lies. The lies.

I tossed my phone from one hand to the other. Over and over. What could Dad do now anyway? Marc was gone. He had to still be in Calgary somewhere because how would he get out of the city at this late hour? I was almost ready to call, had the words on the tip of my tongue to say, when Coach Stu approached.

"Jax, you're still here?"

"I'm staying," I said. "Until Rob's parents arrive."

"You really want to do that?"

"I have to."

He rested his hand on my shoulder and nodded. "Okay. Call me if there are any changes. I have to head home now. My wife works in the morning and I need to take care of our children." He closed his eyes for a second and exhaled a big breath. When he opened them he said, "I can't imagine how Rob's parents are feeling. I know why they've chosen to drive here in the middle of the night. My wife and I would do the same for our children."

"I'll call for sure," I said.

"You're a good kid, Jax. Both you and Rob are role models for my children."

When he left I slouched in my chair. After tonight, I wouldn't be a role model for anyone. Why did some kids end up with two good parents, and others with one, then some others with none? I always considered myself lucky because I had my dad. My mom would never come in the middle of the night for me. The only thing that mattered to her was the next drink.

I shoved my phone in my pocket. Dad didn't deserve this kind of call in the middle of the night. Maybe I could handle this for him. I'd always tried to handle Marc before. When my mind was clearer and I could better answer his questions, I would call Dad.

I pulled out the card the cop had given me and ran it through my fingers a few times. The truth needed to be told. Maybe if I called this policeman before calling Dad, the situation would be easier for him to handle. At least one son would have told the truth.

I was about to press the numbers of the cop's cell phone when Carrie came back with the coffees. Once again I shoved the card back into my pocket. Later.

I was stalling because I didn't want to tell on Marc. I really didn't.

Carrie handed me my coffee and sat beside me. We sipped our coffees but barely talked. Everything was so confusing, and I guess I didn't want to talk to anyone for fear I would say something that would lead to something else. I didn't need her company, or want it either, but she was here with me anyway. This relationship stuff was new to me and a bit confining. She asked me a few questions, but not many, and I replied with one-word answers. Mainly she talked about Rob and how she hoped he got better and what a good guy he was. She also spent a lot of time on her phone, texting everyone, because they had heard and wanted information on Rob.

After about an hour she turned to me. "I have to go. Mrs. Sanford told me to be home by one."

"Yeah, for sure," I said. "I'll walk you to your car."

"Are you staying here tonight?"

"Yeah. I can't leave until his parents come. Mrs. Marino said it was okay."

She took my hand in hers and kissed the back of it. "You're a good friend."

Not that good.

"Thanks for, uh, sitting with me," I said awkwardly.

Outside, the snow was still falling from a blackened sky. I swung Carrie's hand as we walked. When we reached her car and saw the snow covering it, I asked, "Where's your brush? You get it started and I'll clean it off for you."

She tilted her head and gave me a little smile. "Always the nice guy, eh, Jax."

Not really. Not tonight. Tonight I was a liar like my brother.

I took the brush from Carrie and swept all the snow onto the ground while she got into the car and warmed it up. When I was done, she rolled down her window and blew me a kiss. "Are you going to be okay?"

"Yeah."

"See you tomorrow." She rolled up her window and drove away.

With my hands shoved deep in my pockets and my head down I walked slowly back to the emergency entrance. As I walked I looked at my footprints in the snow. Marc's would have been covered over. He would probably think he was lucky.

I wondered if he was still outside. He cold he would be if he was. Had he found a safe place to hide until morning? Or had his *friends* found him? Marc had always been persuaded to do things by other people.

At the automatic doors I stomped my feet before I went inside and back into the ICU. The place gave me the creeps, almost as if I could smell death. Most likely someone *would* die in here tonight. I just hoped it wasn't Rob. This was where all the accident patients went and the people who got in fights and were stabbed and shot. Without looking at anyone I made my way to Rob's bed.

There was no change. He still had his eyes closed and was breathing with a ventilator and surrounded by machines. I pulled up a chair and sat down beside him. And I talked to him. I told him about the fresh snow again and I told him that Carrie had been to visit. I told him that we needed to go to the hill tomorrow.

And I told him about my brother.

"We used to ride our bikes to the river," I said. "Marc was the best fisherman. He had this way with fish. He could sense where they were. He taught me how to ride a bike too.

"I remembered him yelling, 'Jaxie, you're amazing! You got it first time!' I'd always had good balance. I bet you did too when you were little. That's why we're good on our boards."

I'm not sure how long I talked but I kept rambling. I told him all the good things about Marc. Not the bad. No nurses came to kick me out so I just stayed beside Rob and talked, telling him story after story about Marc and me. My eyes got droopy as time went on and I finally stopped talking. I must have fallen asleep in the chair because I jumped when I felt a hand on my shoulder. I looked up.

"Mrs. Findley," I said, running my hand through my hair and wiping the drool from my mouth. Her eyes were a red mess. Mr. Findley stood on the other side of the bed and he had Rob's hand in his. He kept patting it, over and over.

"Oh Jax," she said. "I didn't mean to scare you. You should go home."

"Are there any changes?" I glanced at Rob.

She eyed Rob and sighed. "Not yet. But we're still hopeful." She touched Rob's cheek and stared intently at him. "The brain's not swelling so that's a good thing." She pushed a strand of hair off his forehead.

I nodded. "That is good."

She turned back to me. "Please, go home. You can come see him again tomorrow. Maybe by then he'll be awake."

They needed time with their son. Alone time. How awful for them. My dad always said that the call in the middle of the night was a parent's worst nightmare. The drive to Calgary from Rossland in the dark would have been the worst drive of their lives. But they had made it for their boy.

The devastation on their faces was more than I could handle. I lifted my hand to say goodbye, then walked as fast as I could out of the ICU. As soon as I stepped through the door, I leaned against the wall and forced myself to inhale and exhale. Again and again.

What a horrible place for Rob to be.

How awful for his parents.

I couldn't do this anymore. Keep the secrets. I had to tell someone and I knew exactly who I had to tell. I yanked the cop's card out of my pocket as I made my way to an exit. As soon as I stepped outside I pressed the numbers, and my shaking fingers had nothing to do with the cold. I waited and listened to the ringing.

"Constable Peters." He sounded so authoritative.

"It's, uh, Jax. From earlier tonight. At the Marinos'."

"What can I do for you?"

"I know who hit Rob Findley with the snowboard."

"Continue."

"My brother, Marc."

"Why didn't you tell me this earlier?"

"I'm sorry. I'm so sorry. I didn't want to get him in trouble."

There was silence on the other end of the phone, then, "Are you sure you just didn't want to get *yourself* in trouble?"

"What? No? He's my brother. I don't want him to go to jail."

"So you thought lying to a police officer would be okay."

"I don't know why I lied. I'm sorry." I wasn't saying the right things and I needed to explain myself better.

"He's my brother," I continued, "and I didn't want to tell on him and get him in trouble."

There was another silence. I should have called my dad first. He would have helped me. Told me what to say. Why had I done this? Why hadn't I told the truth in the beginning?

"You and I have a lot to talk about," said Constable Peters at last. "Perhaps you'd like to come down to the station and give a statement."

CHAPTER TEN

I ran to my car, started it, and called my dad's cell. When he didn't answer I called again.

Pick up. Pick up.

It would be seven in the morning in Montreal. He was probably out for his run or in the shower. Then I tried Serena, but her cell phone wasn't on and my call went straight to voice mail. And I tried the home phone. No answer there either.

I had no idea what to do. Now I had to meet with the police; I had no choice. My heart hurt for Marc, ached like an open wound, and I wondered where he was. What if he was lying in a snowbank somewhere? I'd phoned and squealed on him and that was something I'd never done. Dad always said I had a face of stone and a tongue as stubborn as a mule.

Now, I'd talked to a cop and if I didn't go in, it would look bad on both of us. I put my car in reverse and drove slowly down the empty streets. It took me twenty minutes to arrive at the police station. Fully expecting the place to be noisy and crazy like the police stations in the movies where drug addicts and street workers screamed at one another, I was surprised at how quiet it was. I walked up to the desk and asked for Constable Peters.

"Your name?"

"Jax Barren."

"Take a seat. I'll get him for you."

I sat in the chair beside the little end table, picked up a dog-eared magazine from the table, and leafed through it. Without reading one word, I put it down and pulled out my phone. It was four in the morning and I honestly felt as if I was in a really bad dream. Guaranteed tomorrow afternoon when I was teaching, I'd be tired. I couldn't think about that now.

Five minutes later Constable Peters came out from behind the desk.

"Mr. Barren. Thanks for coming in. Follow me."

I did as I was told and followed him down a hall and into an area of the police station you couldn't see from the front. Then I was led into what must have been an interrogation room — it looked exactly like the ones on the crime shows. There was nothing but a table and a couple of chairs and what I figured was a one-way mirror. The female officer sat on one of the chairs. She stood when I walked in and gestured for me to sit in the chair across from her.

On television this is when the actor asks for a lawyer.

"Can I get you some water?" she asked with a kindness to her voice that I liked. "Or a coffee?"

"Water is fine," I said.

Constable Peters put his hands on the table and interlaced

his fingers. "You have the right to an attorney because you are giving a sworn statement."

"I don't need one," I said. I was going to tell the truth now. Why would I need a lawyer?

"We will tape your statement so we have it on record."

I nodded and accepted the water bottle from the female cop. "Thank you," I said.

She nodded, sat down, and pressed the record button.

After giving the date and a bunch of info that was obviously for their records, Peters looked directly at me and said, "In your words, tell us what happened."

I proceeded to tell the story again, only this time when I got to the part in the garage I told them exactly what had occurred. How I had seen Marc trying to steal the snowboards and how he thought they were worth so much money and then how Rob had run in and tried to stop him.

"He didn't mean to hurt Rob," I said in a low voice. "He was stoned and drunk and just reacted, which made him do something really stupid."

"Rob Findley is fighting for his life right now," said the female cop. "I'd say Marc did something more than really stupid. What he did is a crime. You realize if your friend dies, your brother could be charged with murder."

I looked down at my hands, my nails. I couldn't speak.

Please, don't die, Rob. Please.

"So, Jax," said Peters, "inside the house, while all of this was going on in the garage, the other men were stealing things."

"I think so. I never saw them take anything though.

That's why Rob came to the garage to get me. He said they'd taken the television and gone into Mr. and Mrs. Marino's room."

The female cop eyed me. So far she'd been really nice — the good cop. "They took a lot of expensive jewellery," she said. "In fact one of the rings is an old family heirloom and worth thirty thousand dollars."

Thirty thousand dollars!

"Do you think you'll catch them?" My voice squeaked and I thought I sounded like I was five years old again.

"We're working on it," said Peters. "We have some good leads." He leaned back and tapped his pencil on the table. The noise irritated me. "We'll be putting out a warrant for your brother's arrest."

I swallowed. What had I done? Now there would be police looking all over for Marc. They would handcuff him and drag him to the police station and he would know that I had something to do with it.

"Do you have any idea where your brother is?" Peters asked me. That accusatory tone was back in his voice.

I shook my head. "He ran out the back door of the garage."

The cop pushed his chair back, and the scraping noise echoed off the drab grey walls. Then he switched off the tape recorder and leaned forward until his forehead was almost touching mine. I could feel his breath on my face. My skin prickled. My heart started to race.

"I bet you know where he is." He spit his words at me.

"I don't." I vigorously shook my head. I wanted to push back but I was too afraid.

"Not only are you drunks, you're liars too."

"I, uh, I honestly don't know where he is."

"Tell me where he is!" He yelled at me and I thought he was going to overturn the table.

I glanced over at the female cop and she didn't look pleased with her partner. She stood. "That's enough." Then she looked at me. "You're free to go."

"This kid is lying through his teeth. He knows way more than he's saying." Peters grabbed me by the neck of my jacket and lifted me right off my chair. "I bet you're in on it," he snarled.

"You're out of line," she said to him sternly.

"I didn't do anything," I protested.

He pressed his face to mine. "If you're lying I will nail your ass to the wall." Then he released me. "Now get out of here. But stick around. We may need you to answer some more questions. Right now you're an eye witness."

I moved my shoulders around to readjust my jacket and when I did my phone fell out of my pocket.

The cop stared down at it before he eyed me. "Does your brother phone you much?"

"Sometimes," I answered. I picked up my phone, my hands shaking.

"I'm sure he'll get in touch with you tonight," he sneered.

Would Marc call me tonight?

Maybe if I gave the phone to the cops, they would know I didn't do anything wrong. What harm would it do if I gave it to them for a night? If Marc called they might find him and that would be a good thing. Right? I felt sick just thinking that they might catch him because of me.

"I could leave my phone with you overnight," I said, desperately wanting to clear my name.

"We'll enter it into evidence." The female officer took my phone from me.

"I have to teach at the hill tomorrow, in the afternoon, but I'll be around all morning," I said. "If you need to reach me, you can call me at the Marinos'."

"Go home and get some rest," said the female cop.

I tried to sneak into the Marinos' house, and although I tiptoed through the kitchen, Mrs. Marino still came out from the master bedroom, which was on the main floor of the house. She tightened the belt on her long pink robe as she walked toward me. Blue bags hung under her eyes and she looked totally exhausted.

"How are you?" she asked with genuine concern in her voice.

"Mrs. Marino, I'm so sorry they stole some of your jewellery." I wanted to tell her about my brother but I couldn't. Not tonight. I was beyond talking. And neither of us needed to stay up another hour.

"Come here." She stepped toward me and gave me a hug. I couldn't remember the last time my mother had hugged me. Had I been five? Or six? Or maybe she'd never hugged me. Usually I felt uncomfortable when any mother figure tried to hug me, but tonight I let Mrs. Marino envelop me. "Don't worry, Jax," she whispered.

She pulled away from me and put her finger under my chin, lifting my head so I was gazing into her warm eyes.

"We're going to try looking in some pawnshops. Maybe it will show up."

"I can help," I said.

"And everything else is covered by insurance."

"What about all the windows?"

"We boarded them up with plastic bags. It might be a bit cold downstairs tonight." She crossed her arms and tried to smile. "Your window is the only one that didn't get broken. So you should be okay down there for one night."

"The cold won't bother me. I'm used to it."

"Try and get some sleep."

I nodded. "Have you heard anything about Rob?"

"His parents called about an hour ago. There hasn't been much change but they remain hopeful. It's all they can do right now." Her eyes welled up with tears, and she said what my dad used to say. "It's a parent's worst nightmare."

Not all parents. Not my mother.

On my way down to my bedroom, I grabbed one of the portable phones. I hated not having my cell. I would have to offer the Marinos money for the long-distance call.

I waited until I was sitting on my bed before I made the call. This time my dad answered on the third ring.

"Hi Dad," I said.

"Jax. What's up? I tried to call you back. And why aren't you calling from your cell?"

"It's about Marc." I picked at the lint on the duvet cover.

Silence for a few seconds. Finally he asked, "What about him?"

"He's in Calgary. He showed up at my snowboarding competition."

"Marc is in Calgary?"

"He showed up at the hill the day before my competition. He was with a bunch of guys I never met before and they . . . Dad, tonight they broke into the Marinos'." I almost choked on my words.

"They what?" My dad's voice went up in volume. I could see him running his hands through his hair, sighing, closing his eyes.

Suddenly I needed to talk. All the words I wanted to say earlier to Dad just flooded out of my mouth. "Dad, he hurt my friend Rob. Hit him with a snowboard and now Rob's in the hospital in a coma. I think Marc might get charged with something really serious and go to prison. And if he goes to prison it will be my fault." My voice quivered. I couldn't remember the last time I cried. Even when I broke my wrist snowboarding when I was nine, I hadn't shed a drop. Tonight, so far, this was almost twice.

"Calm down, bud, okay. If Marc did something wrong it is not your fault. Where is he now?"

I took a deep breath and exhaled before I said, "I don't know. He took off and no one knows where he is. The police are looking for him. They have a *warrant* out for his arrest. Dad, it's just awful. At first I lied to the police and told them I didn't know who hit Rob, but I was right there and I watched Marc do it. So I just went down to the police station and I told them the truth. I just got home. Don't be mad at me, Dad. I had to tell them. It was only right. My friend might die. Dad, he's hooked up to all kinds of machines and he's in ICU and —"

"Jaxie, buddy, listen to me. You did the right thing. Your brother has to start being accountable for his actions." Then in a low voice he said, "Maybe some prison time will do him good."

"But he begged me not to say anything. Begged me. He looked so sorry, Dad. Honest he did."

"He's *always* sorry. Then he goes and does something again." My father sighed loudly. I could see the expression on his face, the sagging jowls and pained eyes. "I just found out he stole a bunch of money from me and Serena too." His voice sounded dull, exasperated, completely resigned. "He must have used it to get out there."

I sat up. "He took money from Serena?"

"She'd made some cash babysitting and was saving it up to buy some new winter coat she wanted. I think she had over five hundred dollars. It disappeared after Marc came over. And he took five hundred from my wallet."

"That's so low," I muttered.

"Why didn't you tell me you saw him?"

"I dunno. I didn't want to upset you. Maybe if I *had* told you, none of this would've happened."

"I'd like to think that, but he would have done something else." He paused for a moment before he asked, "So you have no idea where he is?"

"None. I hope he's okay, though," I said. "I really do."

"Yeah, Jaxie, me too."

After Dad and I had finished talking, I crawled into bed and pulled the duvet up to my chin, then just lay there, staring at the ceiling. I glanced over at the little window. Marc had crawled through our bedroom window back in

Montreal. I got out of bed, locked the window tight, and pulled the curtains so no one could see inside.

CHAPTER ELEVEN

I awoke at ten in the morning, still dog-tired but unable to sleep any longer because immediately upon waking, I wondered about Rob. I reached over to pick up my cell when I remembered I had given it to the police. I couldn't text. I groaned.

What would *today* bring? Would Rob wake up? Maybe he had already. My head ached and the muscles in my body felt as if I'd had a rough snowboarding fall. I had to phone Mrs. Findley and find out how Rob was. I pulled on a pair of sweats and picked up the portable phone. From the pocket of my crumpled jeans, I fished out the card she'd given me with her cell number.

"How's Rob?" I asked when she answered.

"He reacted to stimulus today. They yelled in his ear and he moved his leg. They told us that's a really good sign. They also asked him to raise a thumb to answer a question and he did. Another good sign. And he's definitely tracking with his eyes."

"Is he awake?"

"He hasn't opened his eyes yet but we're hopeful."

In other words, Rob was still unconscious. I wonder if this was now classified as a coma. I sucked in a deep breath and went upstairs.

With his head bowed into his bowl, Daniel slurped his cereal.

"Hi, Dan." When I saw there was coffee, I got a mug from the cupboard. "Where are your parents?" The coffee was still hot and the light on the machine showed that it had only been on thirty minutes.

"They just left. My mom said to text her when you got up."

I nodded as I added sugar and cream to my coffee. I didn't have a phone. How could I text?

"You want some cereal?" He pushed the box over to me.

My stomach felt like a shrivelled piece of rotting fruit, but I pulled a bowl out of the cupboard anyway. "Sure," I answered.

I studied Daniel. Poor kid. He'd had his room broken into and his computer, PlayStation, and Xbox taken. He ran his spoon around and around his bowl, making an annoying clinking noise. Finally he stopped and asked, "Is it true?"

I froze on the spot. "What?"

Hunched over like a turtle, Daniel poked his head up and stared at me. "That your brother was the one who hurt Rob?"

Although I knew it was coming, knew that everyone would find out sooner or later, I guess I wasn't prepared for it. Not this early in the morning. Not today. I wanted

Rob better first so it didn't look so bad for Marc. "Where did you hear that from?"

"I heard my parents talking. The police are looking everywhere for him. Just like in the cop shows." Daniel put his spoon down. His gaze drifted to a series of family photos that Mrs. Marino had framed and hung on the wall between the kitchen and the living room. Every day I looked at those photos and wondered what it would be like to have a happy family: a mother and father who were married and siblings who loved coming home for dinner on the weekends and for Thanksgiving and Christmas. Last year Mrs. Marino had decorated the house with so many beautiful ornaments I thought I was in a department store. Christmas for me had usually ended with my mother yelling and then passing out on the sofa and my brother too hungover to even get up to open presents. Or he would show up high just when we were about to open gifts. My dad put up a tree and made turkey to make the house smell good, trying to make it festive.

"I think I'm lucky," said Daniel, breaking into my thoughts. "I don't have brothers who would do something like that."

My skin prickled and my muscles tensed. "He's got a lot of problems," I said, knowing I sounded defensive.

"He must have *huge* problems to do something like that." Daniel picked up his spoon again and splashed it in the leftover milk, making slopping noises. His head was almost in his bowl. "I hope Rob doesn't die," he whispered.

"He won't." I picked up the box of cereal and poured some into a bowl, but my hands trembled so much that

I ended up spilling some on the counter. Sweeping the cereal up with my hands, I said, "He's going to get better."

I sat down and Daniel pushed the milk toward me. We sat in silence as I tried to eat my cereal, but the lump in my throat wasn't allowing it to go down so well. Every bite felt like it was dropping to the bottom of a hole. When the doorbell rang, I jumped and accidentally knocked my bowl. Another spill.

"I'll get it," said Daniel.

I quickly grabbed a cloth and cleaned up my mess, holding my breath. The doorbell sounded again.

"Coming!" yelled Daniel.

What if it was the police? I didn't want to talk to them again, answer any more questions, and I definitely didn't want Daniel to see how they treated me. The male cop, Peters, didn't like me because I was First Nations. That was so obvious.

My body sagged in complete relief when I heard Carrie's and Allie's voices from the front entrance.

"He's in the kitchen," said Daniel.

Carrie entered the kitchen first. She took one hard look at me and said, "Wow. You look exhausted. What time did you leave the hospital last night?"

"Late."

"I've been trying to call you," she said.

"My phone isn't working," I lied.

"I wish we'd stayed here last night," said Allie. She sat down on a stool, propped her elbow on the counter, and put her chin in her hand. "We should have called the police right away when those guys showed up at the door."

Yeah, when my brother was nowhere around. Was he sitting in the truck all the time, waiting for the right moment? Or did they go back and get him from somewhere?

"Well, Sophia thought we should call," said Carrie. "Parm thought so too."

"No point rehashing," said Allie. "We just have to have a ton of hope."

Carrie glanced my way. "Are you coming for breakfast? Everyone is going. We're all in shock, like total shock, and we thought it would be good to get together. Then some of us might head over to the hospital. We might not get to see him, but we could take him some things for his parents to give him. I texted and told you all of this."

"I told you my phone doesn't work."

"Oh right." She slapped her forehead. "I forgot. Duh." I knew she was trying to lighten my dark mood.

"I have to teach anyway," I mumbled. At a time like this, I didn't want to do the group thing.

"Not until one," she stated as if she knew everything about my life.

How did she know my schedule? The room took on an airless feel, like I was being suffocated with a plastic bag over my head. "I can't go. I, uh, want to see Rob before I have to go to the hill."

"I just talked to his mom." Carrie came over to stand beside me. I didn't put my arm around her. Last night we had sat quietly and that had been okay. This stuff today about going to breakfast and talking with everyone, going over and over what happened, just seemed too much for me. If I wasn't at the hospital, I wanted to be alone.

"They are running a bunch of tests and he has a lot of family here," Carrie continued. "I guess his brother flew in from Vancouver and his sister is arriving later."

"She's from Toronto," piped in Allie. "And he has that aunt and uncle who live in Banff. His family is super tight, so they'll all be coming."

Girls knew everything about everyone. I lived with Rob and didn't know that much about his family.

"So you won't get to see him anyway. At least not until later today." Carrie nudged me with her hip.

I ignored her gesture. "I don't feel like eating," I said. The excuses were flying out of my mouth. What else could I come up with? What were all my friends going to say when they found out about Marc?

Carrie slung her arm around my waist. "I know this is hard but your friends are here for you."

Once everyone found out that my brother had hit Rob, I wouldn't have any friends.

My brain worked but my mouth didn't. I tried to move away from her grasp. "Okay. Maybe I'll pop by."

Allie stood. "Good persuasion, girl." She lifted her hand in a little wave. "We'll see you in an hour. Come on, Carrie, let's get a move on."

For the rest of the morning, I stalled. Finally it was noon and I went into the garage to get my board. At the top of the landing, I stopped and stared at the bleached-out bloodstain on the garage floor. My stomach soured. I made myself look at the boards instead. That's when I realized the one Marc had hit Rob with was gone. Evidence. I thought of Marc, pacing, smacking his gloved hands together. His fingerprints wouldn't be on the board.

I pressed the button for the garage door and listened to the grinding sound as I watched it rise. Once it was completely open, I headed to the boards, making sure not to walk on the crimson stain. Sucking in a deep breath, I grabbed my board, went outside, and punched the garage-door code. The door slowly shut, locking in the scene from last night, like a drawer being shut.

As I drove down the road, I saw Denny's on the right-hand side, but I turned left to the hill. A part of me relaxed a bit. I was here early enough to make a few runs on my own. I needed that to take my mind off everything. The hill had always been a place I went to clear. And after that I would focus on the kids I was teaching. The whines and complaints *and* laughs *and* cheers when one mastered a new skill would help me forget, even if just for an hour.

When I drove into the parking lot I saw Carrie's car. I groaned. Why wouldn't she just leave me alone? Of course she saw me, because she was waiting for me, and she waved.

I parked and she came right over to my car.

"Are you okay?" she asked. I wasn't even out my door yet.

"I didn't want to go to breakfast." I immediately took my board off the roof rack. When it was loose, I mumbled, "I have to teach and I need to be prepared."

"Everyone was there. It would have been good for you."

How did she know what was good for me? My own mother had never known what was good for me.

I put my keys in the pocket of my snowboarding pants. "I need to be alone with all of this," I muttered.

She touched my arm. "You have friends."

She'd already said that to me. How many times now? My blood felt like it was running through my veins at record speed. "I know that. I didn't want to go," I snapped.

"Sor-ry," she said. "I'm just trying to help you through this. We're all Rob's friends, you know. You're not his only friend."

"I know that too. And we all handle things in a different way." I slung my board over my shoulder. "You may need people. I need to be alone."

She crossed her arms and although her posture was defiant, I could see the hurt in her eyes. "You were okay last night when I showed up. I thought you would be the same today."

"We hardly talked last night, Carrie. I liked that. I can't do the rest of this stuff."

"The rest of what stuff? Me being concerned about you?"

"You just always being around. Having you by my side every minute. I need space."

She held up her hands. "O-kay. No worries. If that's how you feel, that's fine with me."

CHAPTER TWELVE

Faster. Faster.

I flew down the hill, hitting every jump possible and taking as much air as I could and then some. I sailed over to the half pipe and dropped off the wall. I flew up the other side, caught huge air, and flipped backwards. As soon as I landed I cruised up the other side and caught more air. This time I did a backflip with a grab.

It felt good to fly. To be free.

Twist. Flip. Jump.

Over and over.

I could hear people below me saying, "Look at that guy."

After I finished in the half pipe, I sped to the bottom and right to the chairlift.

I had finished three runs before I checked the time; I only had time for one more. I cruised to the lift and ended up riding it with a stranger, some older guy. As soon as I was on the lift, I put my goggles down, hoping he wouldn't want to talk to me.

"So," he started, "are you from here?"

"Yeah." Some people on chairlifts always wanted to

make small talk. I hated small talk, so I didn't ask him where he was from.

A few seconds passed before he said, "I'm from Saskatchewan."

I nodded.

More silence and I kept hoping he wouldn't talk anymore. We were over halfway up when he said, "You've got a nice board."

"Thanks." I wished the lift would hurry up. I looked the other way to stop him from talking.

But no go. "I think I'll get a Burton board next time," he said.

I exhaled and turned back to him. I was going to snap at him and tell him to shut up when I realized that none of what I was feeling was his fault. What kind of person was I to take my anger at my crappy life out on a stranger? He was an innocent in all this.

And none of it was Carrie's fault either.

"They're good boards," I said.

"Which one would you recommend?"

We chatted for a few minutes about his level of boarding and I was able to give him a few suggestions. Finally we hit the top of the lift and I said "Have a good run."

I cruised off, quickly snapped my feet in my bindings, and took off down the hill. Again I flew, almost-out-of-control flew, and it felt good. I hit the half pipe and recklessly dropped off the edge. I crouched low and hit the other side with more speed than I'd ever had.

Up. Up. I sailed upwards toward the grey clouds, wanting to do a 540.

But halfway through I knew I didn't have enough air. I tried to bail and just do a 360, but my body was spinning too fast, my arms propelling me around. Suddenly I knew I was going to bite it. And big.

I landed and the nose of my board dug deep into the snow. Head over heels, I tumbled. Once. Twice. Three times. My board bashed against my legs and arms. I had to get control. But I somersaulted again and slid.

I crashed into one of the walls and that slowed me down enough for me to dig my heels into the snow. I skidded for another few seconds until finally I stopped. I was lying on my back, my goggles all askew, but my helmet still intact. Snow was in my nose and mouth and eyes and it dribbled down my neck.

Was I hurt?

I wiggled my toes, my fingers, and I moved my legs and arms. I lifted my right arm and pulled my goggles off my face. I squinted and looked up at the grey sky, and cold air washed over me. I still didn't get up though. I lay there for a few seconds, just staring at the icy-looking clouds, and thought about Rob and how he'd been stupidly hurt in the garage. Rob would have been better off if he'd crashed and burned on the hill. At least he would have been hurt *doing* something he *loved*.

Would he ever board again?

"Hey dude, are you hurt?" A voice sounded from the distance but I didn't look over, just sat up and shook my head.

"I'm good. Nothing's broken."

I brushed myself off and although I definitely hurt from

the fall, I still cruised to my meeting point to wait for students. Before hitting the hill, I had picked up my class list from the office. No one had said anything to me about Rob and I'd managed to dodge anyone who might know what had happened.

I bent over to undo my bindings and groaned. I stepped out of my board and stretched, feeling pain in more than a few areas. The bruises would show up later. And I would be bruised. Big time. I would tell Rob about my crash when I went to the hospital. I wanted him to laugh when he heard how I'd bailed.

As I waited for the parents to bring their students to me, I thought about Carrie. I had been wrong to snap at her, but maybe I wasn't ready for a relationship after all, for a girl to get close to me like that. My only real love at this time in my life was the feeling of sailing through the air.

Forget about her. Forget about everything right now.

I saw my first student, Callum Abrams, coming over to me and waving so hard I thought his arm might fall off. His mother trailed behind him.

"Hi, Mr. Jax," he said when he stood beside me.

I tousled his hair. "Jax will do, bud. Where's your helmet? No helmet, no ride."

He gestured behind him. "My mom's got it."

His mother had stopped to talk to another mom. I nodded. "Okay," I said. "That's a good thing."

He grinned. "Was that you who fell?"

"Yup. Sure was."

"My mom freaked out in the car. She doesn't want me to board today."

The mother approached us, handed the helmet to Callum, and looked at me. Her eye seemed to move in a nervous twitch. "Are you taking them in that park today?" She pointed to the half pipe.

"No. They're not ready for that yet."

"Soon I will be." Callum spoke loudly.

She groaned. "Why does he have to like this sport?"

"It's fun," Callum answered before I could.

"You should be in the hospital after that fall you took over there." This time she jerked her head toward the half pipe.

"I'm okay," I said. "You can get hurt walking across a street too."

Or even walking into a garage. In all Rob's years of boarding he had never been seriously injured. Bruised, yes. Cracked bones, yes. Injured, as he was now, in a coma, no. Here he was in the hospital because someone was high and drunk and he'd walked into a garage at the wrong moment.

"Well, I guess that's true," she said, interrupting my thoughts. "Callum, put your helmet on and have a good lesson."

All five of my students showed up and once all the parents were out of sight I started my lesson. "Today we are going to work on carving. Going from your back edge to your front edge."

"Are we going up the chairlift?" Isabella asked.

"Yes, we are."

"I'm scared to get off."

"Come on," I said. "I'll help you."

I managed to get all five of them up the chairlift and off

without anyone falling and crying, and that was a big feat. At the top of the hill I told them to wait while I demonstrated the lesson for the day. I carved a few slow turns and stopped and looked up at them.

"Callum, you go first."

One of the other kids pointed to the bottom of the hill. "Look! There's a police car down there."

"Maybe someone got hurt," said Callum.

I turned to see the red and blue lights and suddenly the little bit of cereal I had eaten was sitting in my throat. The lights reminded me of last night and I needed no reminders. Everything was still fresh. I immediately turned, faced the kids again, and cupped my hands over my mouth so I could yell up the hill. "Let's focus, everyone. It's when you lose your focus that you can fall. And we don't want anyone falling today."

One by one, they tried to do what I had shown them. Isabella figured it out first and the look on her face was one of pure joy.

"I did it!" She threw her hands in the air.

"You sure did," I said.

When we got to the bottom, I looked around for the police. Was Marc here? He would know where to find me if he wanted to and maybe he thought this would be a safe place. Had they found him here? I glanced around but didn't see him lurking anywhere.

Maybe the cops had arrested him here at the hill. Could that be? Was that why they were here?

We rode the lift again.

This time when we got to the top, I could see the police

car in the parking lot, but the lights were off. It was too far away for me to see if they had anyone in the back seat.

The time flew by and I tried to forget about Marc and concentrate on teaching. Soon we only had time for one more run. When we were at the top, Isabella looked at me and said, "Can we try to get some air on the way down?"

I glanced down the hill. There was a little jump farther down the hill and they were all good enough to go over it and try to get just a bit of air. Their boards would barely leave the ground, but it would make them feel as if they were flying.

"Follow me," I said. We boarded down the hill and they all tried to carve. Just before the jump, I stopped and they all stopped too. "See that little jump?" I said. "It will be perfect for you guys. I'll go first. Just watch me."

I went slowly toward the jump and caught just the tiniest bit of air. Then I stopped and faced them. "I'll wait here!" I yelled.

Isabella went first and when she flew over she landed perfectly. "That was so fun!"

They were all successful and exhilarated. I remembered my first time. Then I wondered about Rob. When had he first started catching air? Suddenly I deflated because the reality of my life was back, bugging my brain. My hour was up and I would have to go back to a situation I didn't want to go back to.

We cruised to the bottom of the hill and the kids all circled me. A few hugged me. I playfully knocked them on their helmets. "You guys were great today," I said. "See you next week."

"There's two policemen coming over here," said Callum.

I turned to see that Callum was right. And they were heading straight for me. It was Constable Peters, but he was with a different cop. Not the female cop. My throat clogged and I felt as if I couldn't breathe.

"Jax Barren," he said as soon as he approached my little group. I didn't like the glint he had in his eye. Something was up and it wasn't good. Did they have Marc?

"Yeah." I eyed them. Peters knew me; we'd talked last night. Why was he saying my name like that?

He pulled out his handcuffs and yanked my arms behind my back. "You're under arrest for aggravated assault and burglary."

CHAPTER THIRTEEN

The kids stared at me with their mouths wide open, as their parents rushed over to get them away from me. The cop pushed me forward and I almost stumbled. People spoke under their breaths and whispered to one another.

"Wonder what he did?"

I quickly discovered that there was a fascination with someone who was being hauled off by the cops. Everyone wanted to know why.

As we walked the cop told me my rights. I had the right to know why I was being arrested or detained. I had the right to remain silent. I had the right to talk to my parents and/or a lawyer. I had the right to have a lawyer and to be represented by the lawyer as quickly as possible.

The words became a jumble and all I could think of was calling my dad.

Once they were finished talking I said, "What about my board?" I tried to look back to get a glimpse of it. My Burton board. My prized possession. The sum of my hard work. I could kiss my sponsorship goodbye now.

"What about it?" Peters said.

I was flanked by the two cops, each one holding an arm, walking me forward. My heart was speeding like a helicopter propeller and my cheeks felt as if they were on fire. It wasn't like I would run. Why did they have to make me look like a criminal?

We got to the cop car and the cop I didn't know made me turn and lean against the car with my legs and arms spread. Peters told me to take off my jacket and then he ran his hands up and down my body, feeling my snow pants pockets for whatever it is they were looking for. Guns. Knives. Once he was convinced I wasn't hiding anything, he pushed my head down and shoved me into the back of the police car. I stared at the bars and wanted to puke, throw up all over the seat.

"I told you I'd get everyone," Peters whispered to me when I was in.

He hadn't shut the door yet, so I turned to stare him in the eye. "I didn't do anything."

"Well, kid, that's what they all say. You think you can be something, but you're just like everyone else. There's no way out." He slammed the door shut and I was locked in, like literally locked in. I had never been in a real police car and there were no door handles. A crowd grew beside the car, and I could see Callum's mother tugging on his jacket, almost pulling him away so he couldn't gawk.

I slouched and hung my head.

Finally the cops got in the car. I didn't look up. I just kept staring at my feet, my snowboarding boots. I didn't even have proper clothes on. Why would they do this to me at the hill of all places? Now I would lose my job, my scholarship and … what about Podium? Once they found out, I would be told to leave. They had zero tolerance for anything like this.

But I didn't do anything! Except lie. I had lied.

We arrived at the police station and the cops got out, but I didn't. I had to sit in the back of the car and wait for them to get me out. And they took their sweet time.

Finally, after what seemed like an eternity but I'm sure was only around five minutes, Peters opened the door and almost pulled me out.

"I'm not going to run," I said.

"*Your people* always run." He laughed. "Well, *stumble* would probably be a better word."

I wasn't going to win with this guy. He hated me and my culture, and had decided to label me for no reason but the fact I had Cree blood. I decided to give in and figure a way out of this. Obviously Rob had not yet come awake, because if he could talk, he'd tell them that I didn't hurt him.

Peters guided me into the same station I'd been in the night before. Then he flung me around so the other cop could take off the cuffs. He was much gentler and I could tell he was like the female cop and not thrilled with his partner. Bad eggs existed everywhere and not just in *my people,* I thought.

The cuffs fell off me and I rubbed my wrists where they had dug into my skin.

Again I was guided with a cop on each arm. Peters dug his fingers into my arm and the other cop barely touched me.

"I want to call my father," I said.

Dad, I'm so sorry. I'm so sorry. I'm so sorry.

My entire body quaked as I was led to a phone. I seriously wanted to cry, but there was no way I would. I wouldn't give the police the satisfaction of seeing me break down. I had done nothing wrong. I was ashamed of nothing, especially not my Cree heritage. My father had always told me to be proud and be a good person, and that if people didn't like me because of my race that it was their problem, not mine.

Dad. I sucked in a sigh, pressing it down to my stomach. I squared my shoulders. I had to call him.

As I pressed the numbers, my brain swirled with thoughts. Was I going to spend a night in jail? Marc had spent many nights in jail and he told me that "there're scary guys in jail." Once he'd been beaten up so badly, they had to put him in a separate room. He had always told me natives were often targets. Would I get beaten up? I was terrified.

When I heard Dad's voice I wanted to cry, like sob. But I couldn't let them beat me. "Hi Dad," I said. My voice cracked.

"Jax. I've been trying to reach you." He paused for a second before he asked, "Where are you calling from?"

"Dad," I said in a really low voice, "I'm in big trouble."

"What's going on, Jaxie?"

How could I do this to him? He'd always trusted me. Now here I was, just like Marc, calling to say I was in trouble.

You haven't done anything. If anyone will understand, Dad will.

"I've been arrested," I blurted out. For the next few

minutes I spewed out the story, telling a shortened version, as I had no idea how long I was allowed on the phone. When I finished, I asked, "Do you know where Marc is, Dad? He has to help me."

My dad sighed on the other end and it didn't sound good. "Jax, he was just arrested an hour ago at a Greyhound bus station in Calgary. I got a phone call."

"The police didn't tell me that."

"He called me this morning too, earlier, asking for money. He was so out of it I could hardly understand what he was saying. Somehow he must have got enough money to buy a ticket for Fort McMurray. And it wasn't from me."

"Where is he now?"

"I'm sure in a jail cell somewhere. And I'm not bailing him out. Not this time."

Marc was my only hope. Had he told the police I was involved? Was that why they arrested me? My stomach soured. Would he do something like that to me after all I'd done for him?

"Dad, do you think he lied and said I was involved?" I whispered.

"He's an addict. He'll lie about anything."

"What should I do?"

"Don't talk to the police. I'll get you a lawyer and I'll call the Marinos and the school and take care of everything from my end."

"So say nothing?"

"Nothing."

"They said I have a bail hearing sometime tomorrow."

"I'll get the money for you."

"But what about my snowboarding and Podium?" I leaned my forehead up against the cold concrete wall. "I had to leave my board at the hill. They arrested me in front of all my students. Dad, it was awful."

Don't cry. Don't cry. You'll get beaten up if you cry.

"Jaxie, just get through tonight, okay, buddy? Do it for me. I have faith in you. I know you tried to do the right thing. You've always been there for Marc and now it's time for him to be there for you. I will take care of this. And I will make sure we get your board, okay?"

I hung up the phone and gestured to the waiting cops that I was done. I held my head high and sucked in every single horrible emotion that I was feeling, shoving them deep into my stomach. I would not be broken.

They led me to the interrogation room again.

"Have a seat," said the cop I didn't know.

I sat down. I eyed both of them but could read nothing from either of their faces.

Peters leaned forward and interlaced his fingers. "We have reason to believe that you and your brother were working together and you were the one who orchestrated the break-in, which led to aggravated assault."

"My dad is getting me a lawyer." I really wanted to ask about Marc. Where he was.

"If your friend doesn't pull through, this could be changed to a manslaughter charge."

I said nothing.

"Would you like some water?"

I shook my head. "I'm innocent," I mumbled.

The cop leaned back in his chair. His casual body

language did nothing to reassure me. In fact, his body language made me straighten my shoulders and sit up. I needed to stay alert and on top of my game.

"Do you know where your brother is now?"

I looked the cop right in the eye. "My father told me you arrested him too."

"Yes, we did. He was trying to flee. And now he's in the other room."

"He'll tell you I didn't do anything."

The other cop handed me a bottle of water.

"We have evidence to prove you were in on the break-in."

Was Marc talking about me, telling lies? Or was it the red-haired guy? Or blond guy? Was everyone trying to frame *me?*

"I'm not talking until I have a lawyer." I refrained from yelling and spoke with forced confidence. I couldn't let them antagonize me.

Smirking, Peters pulled out my phone. "You recognize this?"

I prickled with sudden heat. "Yeah, it's my phone."

He turned it on and scrolled through my messages before placing the phone on the table so I could read it.

There was a text from Marc. "Thx. Gonna go up north."

"What is he thankful for, Jax? Your help in all this? Were you going to get a piece of the take?"

I looked from one cop to the other. "I didn't do anything. I came to you and told you the truth last night."

Peters stood and glared at me. "You told us to save your own hide!"

I wanted to cower but I didn't. "I offered you my phone. Why would I do that if I was in on it?"

"This isn't all we have on you." He placed his palms on the table and leaned over so he was almost touching me. "You know the red-haired gentleman you said was driving the truck? We have him in custody too, and he said you and your brother *were* working together."

"He's lying."

"We also have *your* fingerprints on Rob Findley's board."

I had picked it up that night. Of course my fingerprints would be on Rob's board. I stored mine beside his and we were always moving boards. And I had picked it up last night, too. Marc had worn gloves.

Peters continued, "So not only do we have evidence, we also have a collaborative witness." He looked at the other cop. "Let's transport him to the Arrest Processing Unit and book him."

I could see the other cop flinch. Something was off. And he knew it.

CHAPTER FOURTEEN

I was driven to yet another building and hauled into a room where they took my mug shot, fingerprinted me, then said, "You will need to be searched."

I could see the smirks because I was still in my bulky snow pants. After undressing, they packaged up my snow-suit. I wondered if Burton would make me give it back. Or would they just tell me I could never wear their stuff again?

Dressed in my Under Armour dry-fit suit, complete with long johns and a long-sleeved T-shirt, I was handed a pair of grey sweatpants. My heart raced the entire time I put them on. My head ached.

Once they had booked me, I was led through a really heavy-looking door. When the door shut behind me I saw the jail cells lined up in front of me. There looked to be around six or so, maybe eight. One looked bigger, like maybe it was a drunk tank. I'd heard about those from Marc. I didn't want to have to march by all the cells and have guys yell at me. I trembled. This was really happening to me. The place had an eerily quiet feeling. Maybe there weren't many in it yet. It was just afternoon. I didn't want to stare, so I kept my gaze on the floor.

We walked to the first cell, and the nice cop opened the door to a single cell. A small bit of relief washed over me. But the good feelings didn't last long. The door clanged shut.

I looked at the cop through the bars.

"You know I didn't do this," I said softly. "Help me, please. You have to get me out of here."

"The truth has a way of coming out," he said. Then he walked away.

I looked around, taking in the drab, cold room: grey concrete walls, a tiny uncomfortable-looking cot, a stainless-steel sink, and a stinky, lidless toilet. I sat on the cot, pulling my knees up and wrapping my arms around them to stop my body from shaking. At least I was alone.

Thoughts bounced through my brain at a frantic speed. What was Marc saying? Would he help me? Or lie like Dad said? He always lied. Always. Did they really have the red-haired guy too? Or was that a smokescreen? A lie to make me cave, give in? On the television shows they did stuff like that.

I have no idea how long I sat on the bed in the same position, but darkness crept into the room as the afternoon light faded. Then the big door opened and I heard voices. Perhaps they were bringing someone else in. I had eaten nothing all day but a little cereal, and my stomach had been growling for a while now.

I curled tighter into my ball. My body felt bruised and banged up from the fall earlier. And stiff from sitting in the same spot. Perhaps it would have been better if I had really hurt myself; at least I'd be in hospital and not in a jail cell. I thought about Rob again. I wondered how he was. I wanted to visit him today. Did any of my friends know I was in jail? Of course they'd know by now. What would they think of me?

Then I heard voices coming toward my cell.

"Jax." A grey-haired man with a bit of a paunch, dressed in a navy suit and crisp white shirt, who looked to be around Mr. Marino's age, stood at my cell door with the nice cop.

I glanced up. "Yes."

The cell door clinked open. "Brian Wilcox. I'm here to represent you." He crossed to the cot and sat on the end of it.

The police officer left us alone and Mr. Wilcox said, "I want you to start from the beginning. And tell me everything. Leave nothing out."

So I did. Once I started I couldn't stop. I rambled on and on, telling the entire story. When I was finished I uncurled my body and let my legs dangle to the floor. I glanced at Mr. Wilcox and asked, "Do you know anything about Rob? How he's doing?"

"I was just assigned the case. My next step will be to visit him at the hospital."

"What about my brother? Where is he?"

"He's still being questioned."

I frowned. "That long?"

"Unfortunately, yes. He's got a bit of a rap sheet. Your brother's in trouble, Jax."

"Am . . . I?"

He patted my knee. "I've been doing this a long time and I use my intuition all the time. You're telling the truth. Now it's my job to convince everyone else."

He got up off the bed and looked at his watch. "I have time to visit the victim in the hospital."

"Tell him I'm sorry," I said, "for what my brother did." Then I added, "And we'll board powder soon."

When Mr. Wilcox had left and I was locked in by myself again, I lay down. I wanted to believe he could help me and that one day soon I would be outside again in fresh snow, cruising down a hill. My eyes closed and I must have slept because I was awakened by yelling and screaming. Jolted upright, I looked across the hall and saw a huge man with tattoos all over him sitting on the bench in another cell. They must have brought some more men in while I slept. My heart raced. This was going to be a long night.

From my bed I only had a view into a few cells. I quickly averted my gaze from the guy with the tattoos and looked into the cell beside him. That's when I saw Marc. He was lying on his back, apparently sleeping.

I left the bed and moved close to the bars. "Marc," I whispered.

"He's gotta sleep it off," said the tattooed man.

"Did he just come in?" I asked.

"Yeah. I think they roughed him up pretty good."

I nodded and went back to my bed. I knew Marc well enough to know he could sleep for hours but would wake up and want that next drink or fix.

The night dragged and the screaming and yelling

escalated, men wanting out, wanting food, constantly yelling, "Guard! Guard!" I shrivelled into my ball again and didn't make a peep. I watched Marc's cell like a hawk, waiting for him to come to life. I had no idea what time it was when I saw his legs and arms move and heard the groaning. I tiptoed to the bars.

"Marc," I whispered loud enough for him to hear me.

"Jaxie," he moaned. "Help me, bro."

So many nights I had got him water, pain relievers, blankets, and so many times when I woke up in the morning, he was gone. Not this time. Neither of us was going anywhere.

"I can't," I said.

"You have to help me," he groaned.

He leaned his head over his bed and threw up all over the cold concrete floor. The smell seeped to my cell. Groggily he sat up. He wiped his mouth, held his stomach, and looked over at me. Even from across the hall, I could see his bloodshot eyes. "Perfect little Jaxie is locked up," he said, squinting at me. "Welcome to the club."

"Marc," I said, "this time, *you* have to help *me*."

CHAPTER FIFTEEN

I woke up early the next morning and my nightmare was still a nightmare. All night I had thought about Rob. Marc had taught me over the years to believe in our native spirituality, so I had spent hours praying to our animals, especially the eagle. I wanted Rob to fly again. At one point, I thought I'd felt him touch me, telling me it would be okay. It was the only good thought I'd had all night.

I looked around the cold cell. What time was it? Would my friends be at school by now? They would all be talking about me. Everyone would know. Even the kids I wasn't friends with. News like this, in high school, spreads like a bad flu bug.

Breakfast came and I ate it, even though it was gross.

I sat up on my bed for the longest time. Finally an officer arrived in the holding-cell area, called my name, and clanged open the door to my cell. I stood up, stiff from sleeping on the hard cot and my fall from the day before. Where was Mr. Wilcox? Shouldn't he escort me? Had he dropped me already? He said he believed me. Had something changed?

I didn't waste any time, however, moaning about my sore muscles and joints or asking about Mr. Wilcox. I made a beeline for the door before they could decide to close it on me again. As soon as I walked through it, relief pounded through me. Were they taking me to my bail hearing? What would *that* be like? I caught a glance at the cop's watch and saw that it was 10:00 a.m. I should have been in biology, learning about the digestive system.

Marc flopped from side to side on his hard cot, obviously needing his next fix. A swell of disappointment surged through my body as I tossed a brief look at him. I sucked in a deep breath, stared straight ahead, and walked off without saying goodbye. All those times I'd helped him and now he probably wasn't going to help me because he couldn't. Just like Mom couldn't either.

"How'd you sleep?" the officer asked.

I looked at him to see if he was joking and was actually shocked to see the sincerity on his face.

"Not great." I shrugged. What was I supposed to say?

"First time?" He walked me forward and his hand on my arm was gentle.

"Yeah," I answered. Under my breath I said, "And last too."

"I read your files. You're that up-and-coming snowboarder."

"I go to Podium." My head ached. *Well, went to Podium,* I thought. That was probably over for me now. If Marc didn't come through I was going to juvie. *Where was Mr. Wilcox?*

"I think my daughter has taken lessons from you in the past. She raved about what a good teacher you were."

He led me through the doors and I saw Mr. Wilcox talking to Mrs. Marino and . . . my dad! He'd come! He must have caught a red-eye flight. Maybe everything would be okay. Maybe he would be able to help.

As soon as Dad saw me he ran toward me and hugged me. I collapsed in his arms. "I'm so sorry, Dad. I really am."

"It's okay, Jax. It's all okay." He patted me on the back. Then he pulled away from me and lifted my chin so he could look me in the eye. "It's okay, buddy. Mr. Wilcox has done a great job."

"We have to do the paperwork and then he's free to go," said the officer.

"Free?!" I looked from my dad to Mr. Wilcox to the cop.

The cop nodded. "You'll be free, son, in a matter of minutes."

Mr. Wilcox and I went with the cop into the area behind the front counter to fill out the paperwork. I had a million questions on the tip of my tongue, but I didn't want to ask any of them in case something happened and they decided to keep me.

After everything was completed and I had a bag full of things, including my Burton suit and my phone, the cop smiled at me. "I have a feeling I won't see you here again."

"Thanks," I mumbled.

Reeling in shock, I walked through a swinging door and right over to my dad and Mrs. Marino. This time Mrs. Marino hugged me, but I pulled back pretty quickly. "I must smell," I said.

My dad laughed. "Yes, you do."

"It must have been awful," said Mrs. Marino.

"Not a place I ever want to go back to."

I turned to Mr. Wilcox, who now stood beside us. "How did this happen?"

"Couple of things happened to clear your name," he said. "First, your friend, Rob Findley, woke up."

"Are you serious?" I exclaimed. "That's fantastic!" Honestly, that was the best news I'd ever heard in my life. But then a picture of Rob stretched out on the bed flashed through my mind and my enthusiasm dimmed. "Is he . . . okay? Please, tell me he's okay. Tell me that one day he'll board again."

The lawyer went on. "He's fine and recovering nicely. He's going to have to take some time off though. He remembered a lot of what happened. Within hours he gave a statement to the police. He said it was your brother who hit him with the board. Now, they did try to fight that by saying he suffered a brain injury, but Mr. Findley insists he was telling the truth. He remembered other incidents that took place over the evening, which were verified by your other friends who were at the house."

Rob would board again. He had to. I glanced around, then quietly asked, "What about the burglary charges?"

"Not a shred of evidence. They have nothing on you. No fingerprints, nothing. Plus, they arrested two of the others and they denied your involvement. They said it was all your brother's idea and you had nothing to do with it at all. They're still looking for the driver of the vehicle."

I frowned. "The police told me they had my fingerprints and they had the driver in custody. I don't understand."

Mr. Wilcox made a clicking noise with his tongue.

"Shame on them. Not true. Well, about the driver that is. And yes, your fingerprints might be on the board but so are the prints of every person who lives in that house. Even Mrs. Marino's. So that evidence would never fly in court. You and Mr. Findley stored your boards beside each other. His fingerprints were all over your boards too."

"What about my brother? Did he say anything about me?"

"Your brother is an addict, son. He said a lot of things that didn't make sense. I asked them to discharge you for lack of evidence and they agreed. I would have fought your brother's statement if I had to, but I didn't. So you're good to go."

I shook his hand and said my thanks. Then Dad and Mrs. Marino and I headed to the exit. When we walked outside the sky was still grey but the cold, fresh air felt amazing. I sucked in a deep breath, letting oxygen fill my lungs. Dad put his hand on my shoulder.

"This will all blow over. I'm going to phone the school today and talk to your principal and your coach."

"Thanks for being here." I almost choked on my words, I was so close to tears.

"I wouldn't let you go through this alone." He squeezed my shoulder. "You deserve better."

"Who's Serena with?"

"She's at the Marinos'. Waiting for you."

"Really? She came too?" My family had flown all the way from Montreal to be with me. Something warm surged inside me. *I do have a family,* I thought.

"She insisted," said Dad.

"It means a lot to me," I said.

We both got into Mrs. Marino's Lexus and nothing more was said until we were driving along the city street.

"I'm so happy to hear that Rob is okay," I said.

"They're running tests on him and he seems to be doing fine," said Mrs. Marino. "No sign of any brain damage. They kept saying if he woke up within a certain amount of time he'd be all right and he is."

"I want to see him today."

"I'm sure he'd like that," said Dad.

A nice silence took over the inside of the car and I allowed it to happen even though I still had a lot to say and a lot I wanted to ask.

We were stopped at a light when I finally spoke. "I really am sorry, Mrs. Marino," I said.

She turned her head slightly to glance at me. "It wasn't your fault, Jax. And Mr. Marino and I knew that all along."

"Thanks for that."

When she looked forward she said, "Mr. Marino lost it with the police last night."

"Really? What did he do?"

The light changed and Mrs. Marino stepped on the gas. "He's Italian and he does like to yell and use his hands when he talks."

I laughed. It was so great to be back in the world again. Her words made me think, though. Mr. Marino was Italian and he hated pasta. I was First Nations but that didn't mean anyone had the right to put me in some sort of box. I was me. Jax. And no one else.

CHAPTER SIXTEEN

Serena met me at the door and hugged me, but only for a couple of seconds.

"Gross," she pinched her nose with her fingers. "You stink."

I grinned. "It's good to see you too."

I must have stood in the shower for twenty minutes. The warm water cascaded over my body and I scrubbed and scrubbed until the bar of soap I was using was the size of a quarter. Turning the water off, I shook my hair and rubbed it with a soft, fluffy towel. I sniffed the towel, liking the smell of clean.

When I went upstairs, I said, "I want to go to the hospital."

Mrs. Marino told me that Carrie and Allie had brought my car home. They had come all the way over to the Marinos', picked up my keys, and gone to the hill to get my car and my board. My dad had phoned the hill and my boss had put my board aside for me.

Serena was watching a television show with Dan, and my dad was on the phone. Mrs. Marino had insisted that my dad and Serena stay the night even though my dad had booked a hotel room. At her insistence, he had cancelled the reservation.

My dad held up his finger for me to wait a minute. So I did. He kept talking and I knew he was talking to someone at Podium. Finally he said, "I really appreciate what you're doing for Jax and how you're handling this. He'll be at school first thing tomorrow morning."

He clicked off and asked, "Do you want me to come to the hospital with you?"

"The school is okay with everything?"

"Yes, they are. They're a little concerned with your sponsorship, but Stu is dealing with that. He's going to call you. You're probably going to have to make a few calls yourself. So . . . *do* you want me to go to the hospital with you?"

"I'm good."

My dad nodded. He understood me and my need for alone time. He always had. Perhaps that's why I liked snowboarding so much. When I was on the hill it was just me and my board. I needed to think. I needed to call Stu without anyone listening to me talk. Was I going to lose my sponsorship?

Rob was out of ICU and in a regular room with three other people. When I walked in he was alone, although vases of flowers lined the window ledges beside his bed. He'd obviously had a few guests. I hadn't brought him anything.

"Hey, dude," he said when he saw me. "Heard you did

some jail time." He didn't lift his head, so I figured he wasn't out of the woods completely.

"How ya feeling?" I asked.

"I went on a little hiatus but now I'm back. My folks are pretty relieved. So tell me about jail."

"I'd rather not." I paused. "Thanks for helping me out, dude."

"I just told the truth. It took me a few hours to remember. Maybe that hit will make me smarter."

"Doubt it," I said jokingly.

We sat in each other's company for a few seconds before I said, "I'm sorry about my brother. He took a real cheap shot."

Rob looked at me and tried to smile. "Is my board okay?"

"Yeah, it survived." I paused, then asked, "When are you getting out?"

"Soon. Like in the next few days. My parents want me to go home for a bit though. I have to take it easy for a while. Not move my head much. I have like a really bad concussion. They're getting all my work from Podium." He rolled his eyes. "Doctor's orders. Something about letting my brain heal. They don't want it to be like scrambled eggs."

"Did you tell them it's already a fried egg?"

"Ha-ha. I'm sure I'll be boarding again soon. My folks are taking me home to *Rossland,* home of Red Mountain." He grinned. "So look out. Everyone will think I'm out of commission, then I'll come back and beat the crap out of you."

"I want to say I hope so, but that isn't true."

"You better not say that. I don't want you feeling sorry for me. Me in the hospital and you in jail, we can't let little stuff stop us from pushing each other."

I nodded thoughtfully.

"What will happen to your brother?" he asked quietly.

"He'll do time."

"Yeah, that's what I heard too. My parents are adamant that he pay."

"So is my dad," I said. "It's been a long time coming."

Rob turned his head away from me. "Too bad it came too late for me."

"I'm sorry," I said again.

"Your brother is bad news, dude."

"I know. I owe you a day at Lake Louise."

Rob looked at me again. "When I come back we will hit every jump on that mountain."

Silence floated around us. Finally I said, "I don't know if you heard but I might lose my Burton sponsorship."

"That sucks."

"I just had a long chat with Stu. I have to phone them and probably write some letters. Thankfully I've got the video. Thanks again for helping me with that."

"No biggie. As for them dropping you, just beg them. Begging is good."

"That's exactly what I'm gonna do."

"You'll be okay. After that last contest, they'll hang on to you."

"And you too."

"We're both gonna come out of this," said Rob. "And maybe the whack on the head will make me smarter.

Things like that happen in movies all the time. Some guy gets nailed and wakes up a genius."

I laughed and at that moment Carrie walked in with a bag of something. Cookies, maybe.

"Hi," I mumbled. I wasn't expecting to see her.

"Hi Jax." She glanced at me briefly before she turned her attention to Rob. "How are you doing?"

"Better. Whatcha got in the bag?"

"Homemade cookies." She held the bag up.

We ate cookies and made small talk and I endured the ribbing from both of them about spending a night in jail. Carrie and I sat on opposite sides of Rob's bed.

After twenty minutes, she glanced at her watch. "I gotta go." She stood and pulled on her coat. "I've got to be in the pool soon." She looked my way. "You boarding tonight?" It was the first question she'd addressed to me directly.

"Stu wants me to take the night off," I said.

She nodded and looked away. "I'll walk you out," I said.

We walked out together, but I didn't hold her hand or try to get close to her. We talked about Rob, but that was about it. We were at the front doors of the hospital when she turned and said, "You don't have to take me to my car."

"What if I want to?"

She tilted her head and looked at me. "Do you think we need a break?"

"Do you?" As soon as I said it, I thought about how inexperienced I was at this kind of thing. I was seventeen and had one girlfriend for all of a month.

She shoved her hands deep in her pockets. "Maybe."

I nodded. "I'm sorry for how I treated you."

She smiled at me. "I'm over that. You were so right when you said we all deal with things differently. We seem to be better as friends, Jax."

"O-kay," I responded. "I'm good with that. But I did think we would go to grad together."

Carrie laughed and punched me in the arm. "You are too funny. Grad is in like months. Here's a deal. If neither of us are going out with anyone by grad, we'll go together."

I held up my thumb. "Sounds good to me."

CHAPTER SEVENTEEN

SIX WEEKS LATER

The powder was at least a foot deep and snow was still falling from the grey sky.

"Should we hit the trees?" asked Rob.

"Let's do it," I answered. Rob had returned to Podium after a month at home. And it was if he'd never been off his board. Perhaps the time off had made him hungrier.

Rob took off first and I followed right behind him. He hit a jump, caught some air, and glided toward an opening that would take us deep into the trees. We dodged around trunks and ducked under branches, the snow soft and perfect. We carved turns, twisting and turning, deeper and deeper.

"This is awesome powder!" Rob yelled. He curved around a tree, hugging it close, knocking branches so snow flew on his face and back.

"You got that right," I yelled back, twisting my way around a different tree. My new top-of-the-line Burton Board moved exactly the way I wanted it to. I had secured my sponsorship with a lot of hard work, a few more wins in competition, and a lot of begging, as Rob would say.

The run ended and we were once again on the groomed track. Rob threw his arms in the air. "That was awesome!"

"Let's do that one again," I said.

He took off flying and I cruised after him, two free spirits in the wind.

We rode the lift in silence until about halfway up. "How was your brother yesterday?" Rob asked.

I blew out a huge breath of warm air and it misted in front of my face. Marc was incarcerated at Bowden Correctional Facility and I visited him when I had time. "He's fine. Working out in the gym there. At least he's clean. For now."

"You think he'll stay clean when he gets out?"

I looked out at the majestic Rocky Mountains that surrounded the ski hill, the stunning landscape that filled me with energy and a sense of freedom. I had almost lost this because of Marc, this feeling of soaring like an eagle through the air. Last month he'd tried to get a friend to sneak in drugs for him and they'd extended his sentence. My mother still drank. Marc was still an addict. Would anything ever change?

Yes, *I* would change. I would graduate and make a name for myself in the sport I loved. Perhaps I would stand on an Olympic podium. And maybe someday I would have my own snowboarding school and a family of my own.

I turned to Rob. "I hope so," I said. "He's my brother. My family."

ACKNOWLEDGEMENTS

Athletes are wonderful to write about because they are so passionate about their sport and they have such dedication and determination to succeed. I'm lucky that I get to tap into the minds of some real athletes to create my characters. I would like to give a huge thanks to National Sport School snowboarder Tom O'Reilly for all of his help with this novel. He answered my many texts asking about different snowboarding moves and he even read the manuscript and made notes for me. Believe me, I needed his expertise. Thanks also to JP Job and Pat Bruni-Job for all their legal expertise. I would also like to thank the team at Lorimer, from editorial to design to promotion to marketing to sales. Within that Lorimer group a special thanks goes to Carrie Gleason and Kendra Martin for all their effort to make this series a success. I would also like to thank the reviewers who read and give me their honest opinions. Your insight helps to build the series. But, of course, my biggest thank-you is saved, as always, for you, my readers. Please read all the books in the series and discuss the issues. And if you get a moment in your busy schedules, contact me through my website: www.lornaschultznicholson.com. I love hearing from you!

ABOUT LORNA SCHULTZ NICHOLSON

Big Air is Lorna Schultz Nicholson's thirteenth novel and the fifth book in her Podium Sports Academy series. Lorna is also the author of seven non-fiction books and four picture books about hockey. Growing up in St. Catharines, Ontario, Lorna played volleyball, basketball, soccer, softball, and hockey, and was also a member of the Canadian National Rowing Team. She attended the University of Victoria, British Columbia, where she obtained a Bachelor of Science degree in Human Performance. From there Lorna worked in recreation centres, health clubs, and as a rowing coach until she turned her attention to writing. Today Lorna works as a full-time writer and does numerous school and library visits throughout the year to talk about her books. She divides her time between Calgary, Alberta, and Penticton, British Columbia, and lives with her husband, Hockey Canada President Bob Nicholson, her son, who plays university hockey in the States, and various hockey players who billet at their home for several months of the year. She also has two daughters who now live away from home, but thankfully, the three family dogs keep her company while she writes.

"Lorna's books are a great read for kids and their parents. They really help teach the importance of having good values both in hockey and in life." — Wayne Gretzky

"Podium Sports Academy gives readers a look into the life of a student-athlete. Through Lorna's books, we have an opportunity to develop an appreciation for the commitment and dedication necessary to maintain the delicate balance associated with being a teenager, athlete, and student."
—Ken Weipert, Principal,
National Sport School, Calgary AB

"These hi/lo books tackle difficult teen problems in an easy-to-read style." —School Library Journal

"a no-fear approach to writing about serious issues that have resonance with real life" —CM Magazine

"Podium Sports Academy takes the pressures of a regular high school experience and dial them up tenfold"
—Resource Links

ROOKIE

I hated this.

I wanted the blindfold off and this to be over. I had a horrible feeling in my stomach. None of this was me. I just wanted to play hockey. *Stay tough,* I told myself. I tried to breathe.

"Let's execute," spat Ramsey.

Aaron Wong is away from home, a hockey-star-in-the-making at Podium Sports Academy. He's special enough to have earned his place at a top school for teen athletes — but not special enough to avoid the problems of growing up.

Buy the books online at www.lorimer.ca

DON'T MISS THIS BOOK!

VEGAS TRYOUT

 It's Vegas. And Vegas is all about how you look.

"You need to lose at least ten pounds." Coach snapped her book shut. "This had better change by next weigh-in. You're the shortest girl on this team and now you're the heaviest."

Lap after lap, I swam as hard as I could to get my frustration out.

Suck it up and swim, Carrie.

Synchro swimmer Carrie doesn't have the body shape that most athletes in her sport have, so when her coach takes her off the lift and puts her on a special diet, Carrie takes it too far.

Buy the books online at www.lorimer.ca

DON'T MISS THIS BOOK!

ONE CYCLE

"Short term is all I want. Maybe just one cycle. I need to get big quick."

"You're sure?" His eyes narrowed.

What was with this guy? Why did Ryan send me here? Did he buy off this guy? He was supposed to help me, not shoot me down.

"Positive. "

Lacrosse player Nathan is smaller than the other players, but fast and a good team player. When he starts taking steroids, everything changes and more people than just him get hurt.

Buy the books online at www.lorimer.ca

DON'T MISS THIS BOOK!

FORWARD PASS

" I curled into a ball. *It was just a kiss.* Nothing sexual had happened.

Then a horrible thought hit me. What if the rest of the team found out? I didn't want this out now. Anyway, what if Caroline said I was making it up? Then I would never make it to the National Team. My hopes and dreams would die in an instant. "

Soccer player Parmita feels the right time to come out about her sexuality is after she's graduated from Podium Sports Academy. But when her coach makes a pass at her, she fears her secret will come out.

Buy the books online at www.lorimer.ca